# NETTLES

# NETTLES

Adam Scovell

Influx Press
London

Published by Influx Press
The Greenhouse
49 Green Lanes, London, N16 9BU
www.influxpress.com / @InfluxPress

This edition 2022.
Printed and bound in the UK by TJ Books.
Paperback ISBN: 9781910312735
Ebook ISBN: 9781910312742

Editor: Gary Budden
Copyeditor: Dan Coxon
Proofreader: Trudi Suzanne Shaw
Cover design: Vince Haig
Interior design: Vince Haig

For Ellen

*'In þe wyldrenesse of Wyrale; wonde þer bot lyte*
*Pat auþer God oþer gome wyþ goud hert louied.'*

'In the wilderness of Wirral dwelt there but few
That either God or man with good heart loved.'

— *Sir Gawain and the Green Knight*

# 1

It was the first day of term when He whipped
my thin legs with nettle stems. The sun was glaring behind the
clouds, and I knew then that I would have to kill Him. I did not
know how or when, but as the stings lashed my skin and my
body quivered with pain, His fate was sealed, cast in marble.

He would die in the Mosslands.

◎

There was the reek of fear in that first week of school. We
had all heard stories of what happens in the first year.
Earlier that morning, the headmaster had said in his

opening speech that rumours of such violence were false.

Our childhoods died in the school. But they would not die in the way that He would. That moment, however, was far off.

The first lesson after the headmaster's speech was Games. It was a mixture of contact sports conducted on the messy field behind the school. We were marched through the corridors and into the damp changing rooms, lit with mint-green fluorescence. They smelled of sweat and mud, even before we had stepped onto the field. The floor glistened with rank water.

Games was first thing on a Monday for the rest of the year, and my first lesson of secondary school. Reminiscence of school always brought back that awful, damp smell and the migraine-lit changing rooms.

The boys looked nervously at each other. We were expected to undress. Our discomfort produced a strange silence. The kits, bought in the preceding weeks by our parents at the school's open events, looked clean and pristine. It wouldn't last long.

The clatter of studs serenaded our slow trudge to the sodden land by the marsh, human intervention there marked only by dilapidated rugby posts. The games then began in earnest.

We ran around the pitch until we couldn't breathe. We were taught to run at each other and take the impact. The stronger boys took to it quickly and soon enjoyed themselves. The rest of us took a battering.

It was a gruelling hour and a half. By the end, breathing stung the lungs. The thick layer of grime gradually gathered from the field was evidence that I was slowly learning to be a man.

The boys were hobbling back after the lesson when a teacher growled an order in my direction. I was to bring the cones from the field. He was bald and round with a scrunched-up face. His cleanliness stood out in comparison to the boys. Mud covered my body and seemed to enter my pores.

My slowness was noted, and I was sent back for the markers as punishment. They were small, plastic discs with a hole in the middle, put down to show the various corners of the pitch, hidden under vegetation and rubbish. No other official markers besides the goalposts were there, such was the dirt. Other objects lay there too: plastic bags, a trolley from the nearby supermarket which was engulfed by the hungry earth, glass bottles, and the odd shoe left by previous classmates after the mud proved reluctant to relinquish its grasp. The marsh wanted the field for its own.

I walked each edge and gathered the dirty bits of plastic, letting the markers drop onto a small metal stand. I thought I was alone on the field as I wandered back under a bridge and through the alleyway to school yard. It was then that He and His boys appeared. They were hanging around the small gully of water by the bridge and were still in uniform as they had cried off the lesson, claiming to have forgotten their kit.

I could not pass beyond them as they made a barrier with their thick bodies. At first, it was a minor humiliation, proving their ability to intimidate. It quickly escalated. One of them pushed me to the ground and the impact winded me. The stand of markers clattered to the floor beside me. It was followed by kicks whenever I tried to get up, keeping me close to the rough tarmac while two of them went back to the field.

I lay there terrified. For a moment, I felt outside of myself as I began the journey into adulthood. Nettles were torn from the emerald marsh where they had been forced to stroll. Perhaps the walk had given them the idea.

My bent knees arched on the dirty floor of the alleyway. The boys were dressed in black, looking almost holy. They wore different clothing to the official uniform: trainers and black cagoules worn under the blazer, with plastic goggles embedded in the hood. The tie of green and black stripes was deliberately tied too short. Their hands were protected by thick black ski gloves.

I cannot get rid of this image. It is a deformity within me. No one else can see it.

They let loose with a volley of lashes. The nettle stems were long and found their mark with ease. The impact from their spindly structure would have been enough to cause pain, never mind their stinging poison. Each whiplash burned and the boys lost all control, frenzied by His encouragement. He conducted them as they slowly moved away, the odd eager follower getting one last nettle-stem crack before they stood by and watched for the reaction on my skin.

He picked me up, my legs shaking. I could not stand

properly. My knees kept inverting in upon themselves as a defence against the growing irritation. Raging lines of red and pink formed in between the drying mud. I wanted the ground to swallow me whole, anything rather than look into His greasy face.

He scrunched my baggy sports jumper in His fist and used it to hold up my scrawny body. I had not felt fear like this before. All previous fear had stemmed from misunderstanding: a scary television programme seen much too young, a misreading of a dog's friendliness as aggression. This was different. I was aware of what was happening, consciously and without confusion. I was afraid.

The collar choked my throat as He applied concrete pressure and brought His other fist up to my face, a key clenched in its fingers. Gleaming metal protruded like a tongue. He said He would Yale me if I told anyone. He dug the key's sharp end slowly into my cheek so that I understood. The key created a precise point of pain, trying to open my face like a lock, threatening to pierce the skin. I still wince when anyone mentions that brand of key. He turned the brand into a verb.

Nothing can redeem this moment.

I rambled pleas. I wouldn't tell anyone, certainly not a teacher. He let the key deepen, enough to leave a dark red mark as I begged Him to stop. Then they let me go.

As I stumbled away, one boy pushed hard into my back with the force of his shoulder, laughing as I landed on the floor again. I was asking for this, they all said, and I believed them. The tarmac smacked the air out of my chest, but it did not stop me from wriggling away like an insect.

As I crawled on the dirty ground, I knew He would have to die.

I was weak and He was strong. I was shy and He was confident. I was afraid of violence, whereas He thrived on it.

Yet, He would die, and I would kill Him.

I left the markers abandoned in a pile and hoped the teacher would forget he had tasked me with their return.

I watch my younger self hobble across the yard to the changing rooms, tears burning eyes, legs stinging, cheek aching. I wish I could go back and tear them all to shreds. My hands and arms as they are now, grabbing each boy and ripping each arm from its socket in swift jerks, like pulling crackers.

It matters little. He *was* torn to shreds.

I was lucky – the teacher could not remember who he had told to gather the cones. Our names were not yet memorised. As I went to the next lesson of the day, muddy, stinking and hurt, I spotted the teacher walking back towards the alleyway, angry at having to return the markers and talking wildly to himself.

The whipping party had vanished into the air. Part of me had vanished, too. My childhood was left behind in that alley.

This was the morning of the first day at the school in the Mosslands.

◎

The train grumbled gently on its journey through fields and hills. I was travelling to my childhood home. Anxiety over the journey from London to Liverpool never eased. I couldn't deny, however, that I missed home and was often glad to be out of the capital for a time.

I had dreams of my land disappearing under marshy water, the River Mersey and the River Dee joining into a single estuary. Most maps realised this daydream anyway, forgetting to include the peninsula where I was from. The Wirral is often forgotten.

This trip was different. Mum had decided she was moving with her partner to North Wales. Dad had already moved from the peninsula to Chester some years before. This trip was my last while still tangibly connected to the area. It made the weekend feel strange and final. Maybe it really would disappear under the water of two rivers.

I sat on one of the train's four-way seats, separated by a grey plastic table. There was only one other occupant, an older woman who started talking after a few minutes. She was from Wallasey too, having just visited her daughter now living in the capital. Initially, the silence between us had been too much to bear and I had made eye contact, smiling warmly. Upon seeing the invitation, she talked quickly, mostly about her daughter's work. She sounded excited about her offspring's life in London, reflecting the exoticism it possessed when telling people from our area.

She asked why I was travelling to Liverpool. I was surprised at first, as – not picking up on any accent – she had assumed that I had had business up north and was actually from London, rather than the other way round. I told her I was travelling to Wallasey to visit Mum. She was surprised, asking if I had grown up there. I answered with a blank affirmation. I didn't sound like I was from there, she laughed. She talked a little longer, her words washing over me, before we dived back into a slightly more comfortable silence. Headphones in, book out.

I couldn't concentrate on reading, as her reaction to my lack of accent sent me back into memories. I had an accent once – the same as hers, in fact, and as strong as any of my friends.

I remember first hearing my voice recorded on a Dictaphone, and feeling shaken by how much it reminded me of His scratching tone. I may have escaped Him, but I had not escaped His world. I carried it with me, even in the shaping of my voice.

From that moment, I quickly and crudely connected things together. I saw my parents ordering food when on holiday in other parts of the country and the changing expressions of people as their accents were heard. Watch your wallets, some had said jokingly in a pub as Dad answered the question of where we were from.

Our accent was locked into this place and people had very specific ideas about what that meant. In my late teens, I made an effort to scrape this remnant out of my mouth. I recorded my voice over and over, picking out which parts of my accent signified the place, marked by sharper sounds, slowly augmenting how my mouth moved around certain words and punishing myself when falling back into my accent.

I tore and tore at my voice until only a hint of the original identity was left. But it still remained beneath the new, fake voice. It was a vocal veneer which required the filing and shaving down of the original teeth. The new, shining teeth were slotted on top, but always underneath were the scarred remains of what once was, ready to be revealed.

With this new accent, my voice would never be the same again. Even people like the woman on the train could be fooled into believing I was from nowhere. I found my voice porous to its surroundings, sometimes slipping back if drunk, or even picking up accents from places I had never visited. I talked in the accents of people who spoke to me, resulting in confusing moments of them asking where I was from, before spluttering my way out of it with painful embarrassment.

I thought my accent would probably revert back to its stronger, earlier self within a few minutes of buying a ticket for my next train, which travelled under the Mersey to the peninsula. I wouldn't mind so much these days if it did. I enjoyed worrying people in London with it whenever they frustrated me, turning it back on as it translated anger more accurately than my bland, fake non-accent. It got things done in the capital.

As the train approached the bright light of Lime Street station, my thoughts turned to the task in hand, the reason I was visiting for the weekend. I wished my visit could have been under more relaxed circumstances, rather than packing up my remaining childhood possessions. There were things in Wallasey that needed exorcising, but I knew much of my time would be spent deciding which toys and books would go to the charity shop.

I wanted to visit all of the old places to see if their spirits could be rekindled, if the old power was still there. I would trap it in photographs, locked inside the small white frame of a Polaroid. I had no vision of what I was going to do with such photographs. But the act alone was enough to shut away the past. Even if it was a bizarre way to go about things, it was still cheaper than a London therapist.

This would be the last time I would consider His fate or my guilt.

After awkwardly saying farewell to my fellow traveller and walking through Lime Street into its hazy underground passageways, I asked the man in the booth for a ticket to Wallasey. Instantly my voice sharpened. I really was back home.

Once on the train, I stared out of the window as the blackness of the tunnel under the river was interspersed with station names – Liverpool Central, James Street, Hamilton Square, Conway Park – until it emerged.

Vegetation concealed Birkenhead's blocks of flats and houses. Piles of refuge sat in swampy looking patches, bubbling beside the railway tracks. The area glowed an iridescent green. I had always found pleasure in this shift between the dated stations and the surprising greenery further down the line. It reminded me of the solace and safety the marsh provided when at school.

The train shuddered as it passed an industrial estate surrounded by reeds, before finally dipping under the M53, its concrete cavern reaching out into a vanishing point of road. My old school was to the right of the train tracks. I recognised the alleyway where He had first led the other boys in their attack. The bridge under which the boys had waited on that first day was the one the train travelled over.

The noisy, metallic rattle rekindled another memory. In later months, there was a strange pleasure to be had standing under that bridge. As the various groups of boys wandered to the field for another round of muddy winter violence, scored by the clacking of studs on concrete, many stood under this bridge and waited for the train to pass.

The bridge was old and rusted. It suggested a time when all that lay on the site were reeds and nettles. Any train passing overhead was unbelievably loud; so loud that certain boys avoided being under it when one was approaching. The pleasure of the bridge came from the escape it provided. Some boys actually enjoyed standing under it as the train went by. The sound was so overwhelming, so engulfing, that it felt as if existence had ceased. Death in miniature was more comforting when a lesson of Games lay ahead.

I remember standing under it once and catching the eyes of several other lads, shivering in shorts and rugby tops as the slow rumbling above turned sharply into a screaming white noise, firing off every fibre of the body with the instinct to run. Our eyes widened with fear and excitement, as if feeling for the first time a sense of our own mortality. One heavily bullied boy was walking under it when I watched him stop and close his eyes. I saw the pleasure he gained from that moment away from everything around him, and the horror at returning when the train had gone.

I imagined the sound created as my train hurtled by. These memories returned in a flash before I arrived at my station. It felt dreamlike to be back, not having visited for several years. Everything I could see threatened to rekindle older memories.

Run-down buildings loomed behind a mesh fence that blocked off the dead land beneath the platform. A lone blackbird scavenged between piles of rubbish for food. The debris thrown there was the most colourful aspect of the place; cans of drink, crisp packets, old condom wrappers and copies of the free newspaper, all comminuted into a thick porridge with ivy growing confidently through it.

The station was a few minutes' walk from Mum's house, and it meant passing the school. I was unusually fearful at the prospect of running into a group of boys, even though I was now much older. I caught myself looking carefully at the time and working out roughly when the next window for them roaming the streets would be. It was two hours away, and I felt embarrassingly relieved. If it had been later, I may have opted to walk through a maze of brick alleyways instead of taking the main roads.

I wandered along the school's road, and walked by the

cleverly disguised suburban houses. It was nice in the day but was different at night. Adult versions of Him existed, attacking stray walkers, holding up florists with stolen police tasers, robbing cars and smashing windows; all stories conveyed to me by Mum, who kept a regular watch on such things via social media.

Soon, I stood opposite the alleyway. I could see the schoolyard. Empty, thankfully. A steel fence was positioned in a two-tier design to slow down cyclists. For the first time I noticed that the alleyway actually had a name and street sign. The passage was called School Lane. It took some minutes to convince myself to go down it in spite of its innocuous name.

My small bag, filled with the bare essentials for a few nights' stay, felt heavy. Every excuse was being offered to avoid this first meeting with the past. Perhaps I could drop my things off and then wander back. It would probably be too close to the end of the school day, when School Lane would once more be filled with boys.

The lane hadn't changed as I made my way towards the field behind the school. The fence hadn't been replaced in the intervening years. My face itched, still feeling the rough mesh pushing deep into my skin, the nettle whip-lines forming slowly through the mud on my legs.

The sky was desperately pleasant, trying to appease the memories this banal place conjured. I decided to wait by the bridge, also unchanged, until another train appeared. I wanted to disappear into that moment, just as

I had done when approaching the muddy no man's land for Games every week.

The field was even stranger in its modern state. It clearly wasn't used by the school any more. The grass was even more overgrown than it had been twenty years earlier. The marsh had won.

Vegetation grew almost to my height. The rubbish was still there, littering a small pathway cut through the undergrowth. I saw a man with a Labrador in the distance, walking towards a small group of wind turbines. The grass and reeds swayed gently in the breeze, sharp bramble glinting in between like broken glass.

I stood above a patch of nettles, their stems forming lines in the wavering mass of dark green foliage. The motorway could be heard sighing on the other side of the marsh. I was gripped by the urge to grab one particular nettle stem that stuck out, remembering the old belief: grasping it firmly nullified its sting. I reached out my hand but could not bring myself to touch it.

I adhered to my plan -- the first instalment of which was a Polaroid of the alleyway. It was all very pompous. I stood under the darkness of the bridge, aware that a train was due to rumble overhead and destroy everything for a few fleeting seconds. Under the bridge seemed the best angle to photograph exactly where I had lain crumpled on the floor. I could see the angle of my body, how the boys had used the design of the school's fence as a blockade against any escape.

The train was close, its sound rumbling through the

earth. I crouched, letting the vibrations pass through my body as the bridge generated its cataclysm of white noise. Just as soon as the train had arrived, it dragged its noise away, the bridge coming to a standstill once more.

Light quickly faded into my first Polaroid, the shadows of the high spiked fence looming ominously as they came into being, casting long dark shapes on the uneven pavement. The moment fell between the white frame of the photograph as I hid it roughly between the pages of a book. I already felt lighter.

There was no period of grace in the school. The nettles were only the beginning.

I sat half-dazed in the lessons that followed, only reawakening when the fear of a teacher roused me. Was this a normal day at the school? I replayed the events of the morning over and over again, wearing out my thoughts like a damaged VHS.

Out of instinct, I hid during the first break between the lessons, which thankfully lasted only fifteen minutes. I initially thought of tagging onto differing groups of boys who had joined from my previous school, but the opportunity failed to arise. I lingered nervously near an old brick block used for woodwork lessons.

I wished so much to be on one of the passing trains, heading under the river towards Liverpool and away from the Mosslands. I would spy a passenger lazily gawping out of the window as the train shot by, filled with ragged jealousy.

I avoided Him and His cohorts; everyone in fact, even a friend I already knew from my previous school. I had brushed him off quickly in my search for somewhere safe. He later asked where I had got to, as if I had performed an unusual conjuring trick. In reality, he only wanted me around to haggle about swapping a rare card in the latest craze, emphasising the 'need' when riffling through the cards; most of which were met by a bored reply of 'got'.

The school bell screeched its repeated three-note riff. Groups of boys meandered with little enthusiasm towards the main building's entrances. It reminded me of a scene from a film I had watched obsessively about a time traveller, where the blonde youth of the future were controlled and hypnotised by the noise of an old air-raid siren. They became docile and walked blindly into a cavern beneath the head of a great totem, where they were destined to be eaten by violent, cannibalistic creatures.

I remember how dirty I felt as I sat down on an uncomfortable plastic chair for the first lesson of French. The mud on my legs from the morning Games had dried and was falling in small, gritty fragments onto the thin carpeted floor. It was as if I had woken up from under the soil and put clothes over my unearthed body. I wasn't the only one, for many had not showered after Games. Our collective smell followed us every Monday. I saw many eyes were filled with a familiar fear – the realisation that this was the routine for the next few years, and was inescapable.

It dawned on me that, for some of my classes, He would be there too. If so, it was likely that He would be one or two rows behind me, working roughly from the number of pupils in a year, the class sizes, the chair layout of each room – which varied heavily depending upon the subject – and the enforced rule of sitting in alphabetical order.

I heard worried whispers of His name already, spoken with the reverence of an urban myth. I refuse Him that today. He is my folklore and no one else's.

With the dawning realisation that He was not some feral creature who had broken into the school, but was there for the same reason I was, the world darkened. I could not comprehend how I would survive His presence for five years. I would have to follow my first instinct.

I had to kill Him.

Our sets for all subjects were based on exams taken in previous schools, so I was already forced into the lower groups for most of them. It turned out He would be there only for French and Games, and I was certain He would continue to bunk the latter. I worked it out later from my diary and the crossover of lessons. We would share thankfully little lesson time.

When He walked into the room for French, the atmosphere changed. Colour drained from the walls, time staggered. I wasn't His only victim after all. Many stared with animal fear. He was late, and the teacher had already made a point of parading us outside the room before allowing us in to find our prearranged seats. He was a horribly strict teacher, quick to bellow at any fault.

Everyone was intimidated by His early act of defiance in the face of this intimidating teacher, His rebellion further apparent from the smell that wafted into the room. He had clearly been smoking. He couldn't help but impress with such a confident collection of misdemeanours, so brazenly exhibited.

The teacher quickly scolded Him, though it was minor, too minor really. I wanted the system to crush Him as it was crushing me, already pressing at my bones with its monotony. I hoped the teacher would collar Him, squeeze the red life out of His piggy stump of a body. But all He got was a telling off.

I felt Him sit down with a thud, knowing that He was surveying the room as He let His body drop hard like a meteor, gathering looks from the other boys as a strange currency. He would be richer than all of us on that front.

I could feel His eyes burning the back of my neck like the nettle stings on my legs. When not tormenting the boy next to Him, tapping his right shoulder and then flicking his left ear incredibly hard when he turned, He was repeating my humiliation on a different level. He was bragging to others about His earlier deed in the alleyway.

It was so effective that He may as well have been whipping my legs again in front of the whole class, and those He was telling dared not do anything other than play along. The image of my body bent over the table while the violent act took place filled my mind. I tried to put myself in His position, a blunt yet streamlined perspective. What form of attack would He try next? How could I escape it?

I assumed that this torment – a floating laughter from behind, someone asking how my legs were – would be the limit when under a teacher's already empty and grey gaze. Nothing else came in that lesson, at least not from Him. Nothing was done in the open.

Instead, it was the French teacher who decided to continue the bullying, finding a weakness that could be opened up for the other boys to sup on. The teachers in most lessons would make the first, deep cut and allow the others to feast on the humiliation. It was really their only way of control. Get the lads to police each other.

The weakness in my case was my surname, or more specifically the pronunciation of my surname, which was sharpened and used against me with such regularity that I soon questioned how it was really pronounced myself.

The register was being taken, but in order to teach us the new language, we had to answer *Oui monsieur!* rather than the more regular *Sir*. The surnames rolled out for the register, a repetitive ritual that gave them musical qualities. Even those who were struggling most could have recited the register back to front by the end of term.

I was distracted from hearing my name called by the pain of my legs, scratching through my trousers in the hope of alleviating the irritation. But I was only making it worse. The teacher, hunched over his desk, looked up and called my name again in frustration, but he pronounced it wrong. I tried to recover quickly, answering to show my presence but he was already standing up straight, eyes prowling.

He glared at me with bloodshot menace. The French teacher was tall and red-faced, always looking like he had been forced to partake in Games with us during the morning. His skin was shiny, enamelled with sweat, and his shirt was incredibly tight around his neck, giving the impression it was choking him; an effect increased by the overwrought French accent he put on.

His glare drew an apology but then I made a foolish error: I told the teacher he was pronouncing my name wrong. He looked up for a minute, flashing into anger as the other boys suppressed laughs and snorts. Anything to help escape the boredom of our days was grasped with absurdly out-of-proportion relish.

Instead of berating me for speaking back, the teacher thought for a moment, looked again at the register, and then asked a bizarre question. He asked me if I liked scones.

The nettle stings subsided as I was slowly made to stand, rising at the command of his hand. I felt horribly tall in comparison to the lads who were all sat watching this unfolding scenario. Their eyes drilled tiny holes in my body. The strangeness of the question made me nervous. The boys fell silent, unsure themselves as to where this was going.

I said I did like scones. I pictured the little bakery further down the street, next to the petrol station which shone brightly at night on the road, and the alleyway next to it in which terrible things were supposed to have happened to a man a few months before. I had yet to visit the bakery and wouldn't for quite some time. It was a privilege reserved for the older boys to leave the school grounds.

He asked me to repeat the word *scone*. I thought for a minute, considering his pronunciation, and repeated it. Every pair of watching eyes, including His gleeful eyes, were inflaming my skin, my cheeks burning as red as the teacher's. I was ashamed but unsure why. This is embarrassing, I thought, as the heat of my cheek revived the pain from the stabbed keyhole He had created.

The boys tittered like birds pecking over landfill. The teacher looked unnervingly satisfied with my repetition. A grin dominated his round face, to the point where it was less a human face and simply a sentient smile, laughing through pink, bristling flesh. He said I used the vowel in that particular case to sound *scone* as *gone* and not as *cone*. Because of this, he had proven how to really pronounce my name. Everyone else in the room took note. My name was no longer my own.

A demented glee rose in the class. It was not just from Him, whose ecstasy I could already feel building, but from everyone in the room. The air was filled with leering faces. A weakness had been cracked open. They had been given effective permission to attack at any given whim, and they even had a grammatical argument to excuse it. There was actually a boy who didn't know how to pronounce his own name. I might as well have worn a dunce's cap.

I remained silent for the rest of the lesson, aware that the bell sounding would mark the beginning of a new level of bullying, even from those who would eventually find themselves on the lowest social rungs of the school ladder. The bell barked and instantly it started. I could not walk around the school without being asked if I wanted a scone. Simply saying my name was enough to insult me. It was like that for the rest of the year, until after He had died.

He made a point of joining in, though kept to the background as we moved between lessons, judging His timing before making the most of the dead space to sneak off for another smoke. I was grateful for His other addictions.

After Maths – a lesson conducted by a thin, confused man whose unfortunate technique for controlling the boys was to go sternly silent upon any interruption, meaning that he didn't say much at all for the lesson – lunchtime arrived along with a new fear. I sensed that He was on the lookout for me. He had singled me out as His plaything.

I meandered between groups of chattering lads, never talking. It turned out I knew quite a number of them from my previous school, though the restructuring of our social circles, due to being spread into the school's three houses, meant that already the bonds between us were waning. They were hanging on by the thread of the current trading-card craze and little else. It didn't matter, as I was not moving between such circles to maintain friendships. My sole aim was to avoid Him and His followers.

I wondered how He had established himself so quickly and how He had gained this small group of disciples, assuming that they were either in His old school, or perhaps even His neighbours from the houses by the sugarworks. His surname was already whispered as a threat among the other boys. Perhaps it was simply due to His stature, His severely shaved head and His bulky persona, all of which looked incredibly intimidating.

I kept hopping between groups, lumping around my large bag filled with muddy, stagnant sports gear. My friend, still desperate for the card for his collection, pestered me a little, offering his lunch money for it alongside the whole pile of cards he had on him. I wasn't listening. The wet clumps of marsh from the morning's Games had dampened the different coloured exercise books given for each lesson. French was a dark, alien purple while Maths was orange like a hazard sign. The damp had curled their pages.

I considered the problem of how to eat lunch safely, assuming the character of a bird that needed to be alert at all times, especially when eating. I didn't have school dinners then. Having a packed lunch mattered very little to me, but on this first day I considered it a blessing. I could eat anywhere, even in some private nook away from everyone, licking my wounds which still itched beneath the dried mud.

The damp odour escaped my bag as I opened it. Stopping behind one of the small sheds that doubled up as extra classrooms, I noted with dismay how horrible this smell was. My bag smelled like a dead animal.

I leaned against the hut, thinking myself safe. Hopefully He was somewhere else, smoking or hurting some new victim, beaten into the ground where we all belonged. But I had been naïve.

Once sat alone on the wet clump of grass, I noticed the mumbling of boys coming from just around the corner. Noise emanated from the dead end by the railway, separated only by giant weeds and another high mesh fence. I could smell and see wafts of smoke, the spectral calling card of those I was trying to avoid.

I had walked right into their domain.

I tried to stand slowly, not making a sound, attempting to stuff my food back into my bag. One of them must have seen me, crying out my name with laughter. The mere sight of me was now a joke. I could have run away, but what would have been the point? Where could I have run to? Running would have made it worse, the punishment more public, perhaps heightened and aggravated by the boredom of young men eager for anything to break the tedium of this new shared life.

I stood still, fixed to the ground. I hoped a train travelling along the lines up the incline would somehow crash off its tracks and wipe us all out. Crush us all, I thought, before anything else happens. My only wish was that I would kill Him. I would sometimes chant it under my breath, hoping that if I could fill myself with enough hatred, it would somehow manifest in the physical world.

I will kill you. I will kill you. I will kill you.

He swaggered up to me and grabbed my bag. He asked if I had any food, the words fired with precision. I lied, saying no. He threw me against the pebbledash of the hut, uneven like coral. It was surprisingly sharp.

He started what would become a regular routine that autumn. He asked again about food. I said no. He slapped me hard across the face in response. My skin turned hot and painful. I was always hot with pain in those school days.

The slap left me dizzy, my jaw struggling to catch up with my head. I thought an imprint of His hand would be left on my cheek, such was the power He yielded.

He asked a third time. I said no. He slapped me again, much harder still. I could barely stand with the dizziness and the pain of the inflamed skin. He wanted to break my will. Perhaps if I had lain down and accepted His authority, I would not have been His regular victim. But

I was possessed of a determination not to play the part, not to allow this to define us both – no doubt a product of watching too many heroic characters in films. It allowed Him to come back for more.

A voice from the ground then drifted through the air and spoke to me.

The voice rose from the earth, reassuring me in its weird soil-language. It was going to be alright, it conveyed in calming, flaky whispers. Take the pain, it said. He continued to slap my face while the earth spoke.

*Take the pain.*

His friend took my bag and grabbed the lunchbox, handing out the food to the other boys. He turned to me again, enjoying himself. Finally, He asked if I had any food, while eating my apple, biting into it and spitting bits of it onto me as He spoke. My eyes leaked salty tears, but I was certain He was aware of an inner resolve.

I will kill you, I thought. The words gained a tangible quality, echoed and sharpened by the soil's voice.

*Yes, we will.*

I responded once more to His question with a no, and He slapped my face so hard into the ground that I thought I would fall through it.

The bell sounded. A crackling relief filled me, knowing that, even with their penchant for being late, they could not keep up this beating. The ground whispered again.

*Take it.*

So, I took it. A final kick from His trainer caused the reflex of my body to scrunch up into a pathetic ball. I watched an aeroplane make its way above, leaving a white plume behind it, wishing I was on it.

He walked off laughing. The boys left with Him, shouting their abuse, but their words seemed to fade into the ground. It soaked them up like a sponge. As I lay there, an unusual feeling of contentment arrived, a calm that choked down the aches and pains.

I creaked upwards, noting the new bruises. My red, muddy fingers mapped my body's injuries. My chest hissed with patches of pain. Each movement felt like touching an electric wire. I was dizzy, from hunger as much as the beating; an empty feeling that hollowed the body. I could not walk straight and was worried that my appearance would raise the ire of the teachers.

My blazer, once black like a deep lagoon, was stained with long strips of mud and strands of grass, as were my trousers. My shirt was still unusually pristine bar the faint imprint of the sole of a trainer. But my tie, with its emerald and black lines, was crumpled, pulled into a tight knot by His grabbing hands. I imagined my face was beetroot red, my eyes were certainly watering, and my hair was ruffled. I could not undo the tie now it was so tight.

I staggered around, trying to make out the low reverberations of the voice that had spoken from the ground. With the stamping feet of boys making their way indoors, I could hear nothing.

I could not survive days of this, I thought, let alone years. I dared not think about the terrifying amount of time we were supposed to spend in this building, with its sick walls that taunted bored eyes with their constant presence. Every inch was there to remind you that you were nowhere else. There was no forgetting that this building was everything once you were inside.

As I hobbled along, I was stopped at the door. A tall teacher, whose name I would never learn, shouted down from a great height about my tie and my use of that particular door. In later years, I was told he was ex-military, and it showed. He was even taller than the French teacher, muscular and aggressive in the way he spoke and moved.

This was not my door. This was the year above's door. He asked rhetorically if I was trying to sneak through due to laziness. His speech was punctuated with a hard, pointing finger jabbing into my chest where He had stamped mere minutes before. The pain returned sharply, and it shocked my eyes into an electrified stare, as if I was about to turn savage and rip the teacher's spindly finger from its socket.

He recognised my reaction but misread it as rebellion. I was only trying to hide the immense pain his trivial movement had summoned, but he met it with an equally wide stare, daring a confrontation.

I manoeuvred my hands slowly around my tie until it was as neat as possible. I apologised quietly and went to the other door. The teacher's eyes followed as I limped away pathetically, wondering if he would question why I was in such a clearly battered state. It was not his concern.

The teacher's scolding had slowed my journey further,

meaning that only a handful of boys still lingered around the corridors, and even then only in flashes at the corner of the eye. I hobbled quicker, making my way through the acrid Science block, which reeked of disinfectant. The History block was at the furthest end of the corridor, marked by a rough, wiry carpet.

I was glad it was this lesson. He would not be in it.

I must have seemed like a ghost who had stepped through the wall. Everyone was already seated and seemed shocked and amused by my appearance in equal measure. One boy mouthed 'scone' at me. I was battered, like a piece of meat dragged along the ground.

The silence was lifted as I was scolded by another teacher, a young blonde woman with a sharp voice who had only recently finished her teaching studies. For some reason, a rumour spread that one of her breasts was made of metal, as one boy had supposedly run into her chest and been knocked clean out. I still laugh thinking of the seriousness of the topic when it was discussed, in particular the supposed *clang* of the impact.

After a few more jokes regarding my name – she got the pronunciation painfully wrong too – I was allowed to slump into a rigid chair, hoping to slip into sleepy oblivion.

I sat in a blur through those final lessons. I imagined Him struggling through a difficult subject, hopefully with an equally difficult teacher who would punish Him relentlessly. But really, I wanted Him as confident and arrogant as He was when attacking me.

I wanted my eventual revenge, which I dreamed into

fiery existence once more, to be a complete surprise. I wanted to witness that moment in His eyes when His confident, boyish character would die swiftly and knowingly. That shift, I assumed, would be joyous, as He realised that I, that weak boy He had whipped with nettle stems, was stealing His last essence of life.

The first day was dragging, even with those visceral images in my thoughts. My eyes watched every minute dawdle by on the clock, hoping the day would end. The lesson was mostly about the importance of covering our new exercise books with wallpaper.

Thoughts of how this was the new normal hung heavy on my shoulders, as it did upon everyone else's. I was not the only boy to be bullied. Many were like me, and each had their own particular battles to face. It was more terrifying an idea, more horrific a reality than anything He could have put me through: the fact of us being locked in together, all day, for years to come.

The monotony of dark, wet mornings, waking up before it was light and coming home just as wintry dusk fell. It was unbearable to think about. Winter would be long. All light would be stolen from our lives, minute by minute. Only the present was left, tattered in an ill-fitting uniform.

I needed somewhere to escape, and I contrived complex and convoluted plans instead of paying attention.

The room for the lesson was at the very end of the school's building, curving to follow the marsh and the train track, joining up to another playing field adjacent to it, all tidy and gleaming green in the last remnants of the season's sun. Only older boys were allowed to use it. It was only the marsh for our Games lessons.

Finally, there was the motorway, which could be seen out of the window on the horizon. It was close enough to hear cars drive by and the occasional rumble of a lorry trundling along its tarmac. It was the first time I had noticed the motorway.

The motorway hypnotised with its constant rhythm. I thought of the voice from the ground, similar in its rumbling tone. There was a semblance of care in that voice, like those of my parents. I could never describe the voice properly, as if it was just on the cusp of my perception, ready to tip over into white noise when close to recognition. The earth had spoken with a voice box of crackling soil, the vibrations of a larynx riddled with stones and worms. It faded between the cracks like water on the field, travelling down into the unknown. But I do remember its first words.

*Take the pain.*

The final bell of the day rang, and the relief made me gasp. There was an audible sigh from pupils and teacher alike, as if we had all been holding our breath. She told us to get out quickly, her head held in her hands as she sat at her desk, exhausted by our company. One boy swore he heard a metal clang as she slumped down, telling us seriously and confidently as the thirty or so boys fought to get through the room's door. No one believed him.

I had been in a dream, my eyes walking through the window and along the edge of the playing field over and over again, especially the part walked brown and sodden by wanderers heading towards the motorway.

Until I stepped through the doorway of my house, I knew I wouldn't feel safe. The worry soon played on my mind as we all jostled to get out. He could find me, follow me, and subject me to more. I was not going to allow another beating. The thought of another round made my stomach turn. But I had other reasons to get home quickly.

I needed to change and get washed, especially after the morning's Games, which had left me smothered with an extra skin of dry mud. I felt rancid with dirt. My parents could not find out about what happened.

I foresaw the scenario if they did: phone calls to the school, accusatory parades in which I had to point Him out, the false retribution He would receive and the very real retribution I would get in turn, at some unnamed point in the future. The illusion that school was enjoyable was the right thing for us all.

There was a set of shining railings that bordered the tidy field beside the motorway, in which was set a small gate. To its left sat the car park, perhaps the only place where, if any trespass was witnessed, a genuine punishment was doled out, because the teachers were paranoid about their cars being damaged.

I gambled as, if He was near, I would be trapped. I didn't know this side of the yard properly, as it was designated for the three oldest years. I was only allowed to be there at the end of the day, when the main desire was to get everyone out of school as quickly as possible. I took the risk, the History classroom being the nearest room to the small gate.

The marshland to the right was quiet, except when a train groaned across the tracks. My bag, filled with damp clothes and curled exercise books, jumped up and down on my back as my steps grew faster, aiming for the gate. The field came into view, green everywhere, green as nettle stems.

Beige council houses began at the far end where the field met the road. I would risk going through the allotments that started behind the houses on the other side of the school's road and concluded on my road. I already hated how close school felt to home.

On the pavement I broke into a run. Only in my cul-de-sac would I be safe. I climbed the allotments' first scraping gate, avoiding its crown of barbed wire and unafraid of covering myself in more mud. I ran clumsily through the tight pathways of bramble and blackberry bushes, my chest heavy and my breath tasting of iron, the words of the soil ringing in my ears.

*Take the pain.*

I reached the larger gate leading to my road, and tore a small hole in my shirt as I climbed over, each breath now molten. I looked around obsessively, checking for any sign of Him gliding towards me in secret pursuit.

I made a final sprint towards my front door until I was locked inside the familiar porch, fumbling with a house key whose brand reminded of the red mark on my cheek. The run had re-irritated the fading stings on my legs and I

collapsed through the doorway, crying with happiness that
school was over.

This was the end of my first day at the school in the
Mosslands.

◎

Being back in Wallasey made me uneasy at first. In some
ways, the house I grew up in was more disconcerting than
the alleyway where I was attacked all those years ago. I
could not bring myself to photograph the house in the way
I planned to capture other places, though the temptation
to do so was strong. It was yellow like memories of sunny
days, too lived-in a place to consider trapping in Polaroids.

A frustration of hills lay ahead. It brought back a wave
of memories: the discomfort of the walk in the summer
heat, the danger spots where gangs of boys would fester
in waiting, the quickest and safest ways back home. All
were returning as I started the ascent up a hill called
Wallacre Road. It was a grey incline and unbearably steep.
A sweeping view, however, was the reward for climbing it.

The concrete of the motorway made unusual shapes in
the distance, the sky partly blocked by bored walls and the
dead plants of small front gardens. At the peak, I turned
back to look over the marshland stretching towards Wales.
The school was hidden, and I was thankful, for the vista
was pleasant in its edited form. The green of the neater
playing field was bordered by a long, snaking tarmac path
that I knew ran all the way alongside the school and the
railway. Then the motorway rose up, growing out of the

land. The ground beyond vanished gently into the haze, shaded on the horizon by faraway Welsh mountains, retail parks and indistinguishable detail that fizzed with small movements.

The view was even more engulfing from the raised piece of green space over the way, but I was not to visit there for the time being. Some places needed more preparation before revisiting, and The Breck, as it was called, was one of them.

I had many dreams of walking along the motorway at night. When younger, I envisioned long highways stretching into the night, emptied of all cars but occupied with the echoing voices of the marshland coaxing me to walk on.

The pub at the top of the hill had closed during the recession, its windows covered with metal sheets, pockmarked with small black holes and scratched with graffiti. It brought back memories of watery beer and two-man cover bands that only seemed to play songs by Bad Company and Genesis. A tatty Union flag hung limp and rippled in the breeze above a stained St George's flag. The bricks of the building had been slowly piled up in a corner of its car park. It was a building in decay.

The trees of The Breck hung over the car park and the road, daring passers-by to wander into its darkness. Beyond the wall of the road was the start of The Breck's greenery, which stubbornly grew out of the area.

I needed to visit Mum's house before doing anything else, and I had already decided that I wanted to see the motorway before visiting The Breck. I would not go anywhere carrying anything valuable other than my Polaroid camera, so I needed to drop my bag off at the house.

I was already worrying whether I could make another visit in time before the end of the school day. I had never lost that strict rhythm imposed during school.

Breck Road, named after the land behind it, flowed in a familiar, inviting way until the curve of my road went off to the right, down another hill. The blossom on the tree at the top was browning from light-pink to coffee. It was a warm season, where summer threatened to continue on some days and unpredictably fall into autumn on others. The seasons were increasingly blurring into a mess of weather patterns.

There was no one about on the pavement, but the road was busy with a variety of noisy cars. This was a place that was passed through. They did not stop.

Sunlight reflected off greenhouses, glimmering through the railings of the allotments at the ending cornice of my road. I walked down my hill and looked at the vegetable patches through the bars of the gates. The allotments looked just as dead as they had done in the days when I fled through them; climbing the high metal gate and walking through tight, muddy paths shrunken further by persistent thistles and unstoppable buddleia that wore halos of colourful insect admirers in summer. The road seemed smaller too, but rather than being due to the growth of weeds, it was due to the abundance of cars.

I knew Mum's partner would be in the house, though I was uncertain whether she would be. I wondered if there was a key left for me under the stubbly mat, a practice unchanged since childhood.

I felt uncertain about staying in the house. Friction is often created when older children revisit their parents, disturbed by the changes implemented and the unusual choice of things kept exactly as they were. Memories rub against the time elapsed since last there.

I could hear a television and knew that Mum's partner was in. The house creaked as I greeted him, his hand reaching out for a typically tight handshake. He was incredibly tall, even taller than I was, often wearing camouflage clothing and bandanas. He had a small beard and enjoyed motorbikes, one of which was parked behind the house and shook its foundations whenever started. I could feel my bones crush in his grip, better designed for working a throttle or a blowtorch when he was working as a welder. He was watching a Spaghetti Western starring Lee Van Cleef.

The house was already detonating memories. Its bowls of faded potpourri; its occasional photograph of my childhood self, smiling; television guides; niche household gadgets; accessories for the motorbike. I needed to escape outside again almost instantly, not only because of the melancholy of no longer recognising the house's intricacies, but because the old rhythm of daytime order had firmly reasserted itself. I knew that the boys would be escaping from their various classes in another hour, and I wanted to visit the motorway before a single person had stepped out of the school gates, drunk with freedom.

My room was still recognisable. Christopher Lee's autograph hung on the wall above my bed next to a groaning bookcase of messy, unorganised paperbacks, a few replica props from the science-fiction show I adored and two guitars silently gathering dust.

I threw my bag on the bed, and took my camera out. The Polaroid of the alleyway had already developed strong colours and hues, the memory locked within. It bulged with time, coloured by the pain of nettle stings. The white frame of the photograph was thankfully too strong for the feelings it summoned to escape.

My collection had started.

There was a picture border all around the room made of three strips of wood descending in level and thickness. It seemed much higher when I was younger. I stood on the bed and placed the Polaroid on it. It was perfect for displaying the photographs, and I planned to place all of them along it; creating a map of past times and places.

The motorway now beckoned. I could feel its pull. To get there would mean walking across the neat playing field.

It was where He had died.

◉

The sun crept through the curtains of my room on the second day of school, as did dread. Why couldn't the night last forever? They could not make us go when it was dark. Sunlight brought my room into existence with a sort of mocking glee. The stings on my leg were now just faint marks and no longer irritated. My body was a dead weight, every fibre resisting getting up.

I took solace that He could not be everywhere at once. There was definitely a place to hide in the breaks between lessons: under the motorway, if only I was brave enough to use it.

Mum, energetic and stressed, ushered me through the morning routine. She called for me to get up, then to get dressed, then to eat breakfast. I needed encouragement to do everything.

She was sat in her grey trouser suit, talking quickly on her phone to security men in Liverpool as I sat moping at a table in front of a bowl of crackling cereal. I did little except push it around with a spoon. Lads in Speke had set fire to a house and then shot fireworks at the arriving fire engine. Her job had been to secure the empty building with steel shutters, but the lads had somehow got in anyway. Angry men were shouting at her through the tiny speaker of her Nokia as she tried to eat a soggy piece of toast.

For a moment, I thought she would notice my quietness. But her phone never stopped, the angry voices continuing to ask what was being done. As she rang Jimmy, her work colleague, she asked quickly if I was feeling unwell, putting the back of her hand to my forehead. I told her no but that I hated secondary school. She smiled and said I would get used to it, before she stood up to take another call. Her phone was relatively new, given to her by the security company where she worked in sales. It was a tough job surrounded by tough people, especially the security men themselves who all seemed to be ex-mercenaries, debt collectors or ex-criminals. They were all terrified of her.

Dad had left the house before I was awake, as he cycled to the hospital in Birkenhead where he worked in one of the laboratories. Mum called out a pleasant goodbye as the door closed behind her and I sat limp and silent at the table, her voice fading as she walked to her car.

I had managed to wash my uniform by hand before either parent had noticed the muddy marks. It felt stiff as I had secretly dried it on a radiator. The jacket was especially oversized, like all uniforms seem on first-years, emphasising how childlike I still was.

It occurred to me that my parents were very trusting in leaving me to go to school alone and not waiting to actually see me leave, especially as I only seemed to get up in order to put on a VHS of the science-fiction show I was obsessed with. It was more important than anything else.

They did not know what I was to face each day in those first few weeks, so they never considered any possibility of my truancy.

The chair I was sat on had never felt so comfortable and welcoming, daring me to stay and continue watching the fantastical adventures playing out on the television. But I remembered the discipline doled out to others for misdemeanours the day before, and I soon hauled my body from its position and ejected the tape.

What was going to happen today? The question tormented me as I skittishly made my way to school. It was raining lightly despite the sunshine, and I was wearing an awful waterproof coat which instantly marked me out as a potential victim with its childish colours.

He must not find me, I thought.

I arrived at the school after dawdling along the road, and haunted the outer perimeter of the yard. My year group lined up for registration and I made a point of staying in sight of any possible teacher. He would not touch me in front of a teacher. He was a coward.

Once inside, I noticed the pleasing view seen through almost all of the classroom windows. The view was bittersweet – the potential escape it provided jarred with the tedium of lessons. This is what we really learned in school: the patience required for future work, watching the days trickle by.

My form teacher read our names for the register. Two boys had already not bothered to come in for the second day. I was jealous of whatever strength they had that gave them the confidence to avoid all this. The form teacher was a young man who wore incredibly shiny ties and considered himself one of the lads. He possessed an estate agent's angst to be liked, and would happily hear the boys taking the piss out of the other teachers without punishing them.

Asking about our first day in the dead-time between morning form and our first lesson, the form teacher gave us advice and told us jokes. My Maths teacher, it turned out, had the unfortunate nickname of Scratch & Sniff, a name which made my form teacher snort with laughter.

The windows were tinted grey, the glass deliberately marked to dilute the strong sunlight in summer. This meant the early autumn weather outside seemed doubly grim, the windows pre-empting the misery of the coming winter. Every movement outside was of interest, anything to distract us from exercise books or the whiteboard with its strong-smelling squeaky pens.

The thought of Him crept into my mind, but so did the voice that had whispered from the ground the day before. I looked towards the motorway, which could just be seen from the window of the English class as we began learning about *Twelfth Night*, which no one found remotely funny or vaguely understood. Our teacher wanted to push us into the deep end, apparently.

The horror of having to read aloud was shared by everyone. Shakespeare was at least a democratic torment. All hierarchies were removed by the embarrassment of having to read in front of our fellow pupils, especially as it was a play that asked us to perform more feminine roles. If we did well, we were to be victims of our peers. If we failed, we were to be victims of the teacher.

It was worse for the harder boys. The English teacher, a stern woman with incredibly intimidating round eyes and bouffant hair, seemed to enjoy giving them the more outrageous parts. One boy, a friend of His as it happened, stormed out at the mere idea of being forced to read a girl's part. The teacher let him go after he had kicked the door, calling him back several times, and merely saying that he would regret it later.

The mood was dark as our first break of the day arrived. Much to my relief, the rain tapping on the windows had forced the break to be taken indoors. We were supervised by teachers in various classrooms, all looking frustrated at effectively having to work during their break. I hid again in the huddles of boys, doing my best to disappear, not to raise my head even slightly. I was lucky the morning breaks were short. No sooner had I found a rhythm to my hiding than the bell sounded and lessons rolled on.

I was grateful that the next lesson was Art, one I thought I could enjoy, but also because the room it was in sat at the top of a raised block detached from the main building. It meant getting a better view out over the motorway and the marshland. The teacher wasn't normal, either. He was lanky, openly smoked during breaks and played us music.

He would sit in his crumpled suit, and sometimes his parka if he was cold, with his Doc Martens perched on the table. He nodded along to the music as he taught, mostly strange bands from the 1960s and 1970s, occasionally walking around to see if we were following his various instructions.

Sat at long, connected desks, he first played us 'Eleanor Rigby' on a CD player and told us to respond to it on a large piece of paper with charcoal. He linked it to a photograph of a sculpture which I learned years later was by Sarah Lucas; an effeminate figure whose body was made out of old stockings, sat on an intimidating wooden stool.

I had never heard anything like it or seen anything like the sculpture, though I soon drifted and daydreamed of the marsh once more, just as the strings ended after the final chorus of all the lonely people.

Next, he played 'Lady Madonna' very loudly. He wanted to contrast different emotions and have us respond visually, showing us a surreal painting by Salvador Dalí of a woman with a bouquet of roses for a head. It was all about sex, apparently. The music made for a strange comparison as I sat watching the cars fly over the motorway in the distance, letting my eyes wander under the bridge, as far along the path as I could see before the view was blocked by the bullying structure of the road.

I could hear the song finishing, and so quickly scribbled some symbols that I assumed to be carefree before fading back into the view of the road. I had walked there with Dad a few times looking for reed warblers when I was younger, and I could picture the unusual metal bridge that had been installed over the railway lines, replacing an old concrete one. The marshland possessed my thoughts, as if plant life was sprouting in my mind. Its teasels and weeds expressed a strange sentience.

The urge to walk out of the class and wander into its green beating heart was palpable, though dampened by fear of punishment.

Even in the more bearable classes, there was still an undertone of general bullying, and not just of me for my name and obvious physical weakness. One boy was short and round, which led to a campaign against him that was far more severe than mine. It lasted years. I assumed he had already been marked as a target by several of the other boys roaming the corridors. He sat at the end of the table, furiously scribbling as a diversion from taunts whispered by the boys around him.

Lunchtime was approaching and an uncharacteristic determination took hold. My eyes met with those of the round boy and for a moment we shared our fear, knowing what was to come. I hadn't shared a class with Him since French, and assumed my calculations had been wrong about where He was placed. Aside from French and Games, He was kept apart in a special class for the majority of the time.

Whereas most of the boys were placed in the houses of Faraday, Ruskin or Grenfell – the latter being mine, with a tie demarcated by a red stripe among the black and green – He was in a class simply marked with an M. He was one of the Ms, the most volatile and violent pupils in the school. They intimidated by reputation alone. He and at least two of His mates from the Ms would be in French and Games as part of a development programme to integrate them with their peers. It was deemed improper to let them near the other pupils for most lessons, though this went out the window at break times.

For lunchtime, I decided to keep on the move rather than find somewhere to hide. My determination had quickly fizzled away, as the small gate leading to the adjacent playing field was guarded by a teacher checking pupils coming and going. I could not attempt to get to the motorway, as it was still uncertain whether the weather would change, meaning teachers would bring everyone back in again. But we were allowed out as the morning showers had subsided.

I saw Him with His gang at one point, sneaking towards the rear field down the alleyway, I assumed to smoke. I felt a heavy relief. Perhaps that first day of violence was simply a one-off. My confidence was to prove naively unfounded, though it was an overwhelming feeling as the bell rang after an hour of empty worry.

I lingered behind, developing a slow gratitude for the horrible noise from the bell, denoting that I had survived another social obstacle course.

I needed to use the toilets, but was already thinking twice about entering them. Until that point, I had avoided doing so, as they had quickly become infamous. The cubicles had no locks or paper, only incredibly heavy metal doors painted red which, I would soon learn, could be kicked from the outside with great velocity. The cubicles were the only sensible option, however, as the boys quickly developed a habit of bending their knee behind yours, meaning you could lose balance and piss on your own legs. The cubicle was the only choice, and its flying metal door was, at least, not guaranteed. It was a bad decision either way, however, because not long after I had entered, He came in.

I knew it was Him as I heard His voice laughing along with the familiar echo of His followers. I felt the world drop several shades in colour, feeling faint before the adrenaline knocked my daze away and replaced it with a jittery, nervous static between my ears.

I tried to conjure the voice from the ground, hoping it would visit again to whisper its words of comfort. The nettle stings itched as if they were a permanent mark of His presence, a forewarning. But I could neither run nor escape. It could only be a quick beating, a humiliating but short moment before the inevitability of the day's final classes dragged them away.

I stood facing the red door of my cubicle, expecting it to fly open, pre-empting the powerful force that its weight gave to even the slightest kick. There was a quiet stillness as I waited, hoping to hear them leave. Then the kick came and the door slammed past, catching my arm. The glee on His face filled me with horror. Not only had He found someone to torment, but He had found *me*. I was clearly His favourite.

The possibility of continuing His bullying rather than starting afresh with a new victim gave Him a relish for His work. I fail to recall what He said as He dragged me out and pushed me into the circle of other boys. I felt my body go dead, a defensive reflex as jabs and kicks found their mark.

He strode into the circle, pulling something from His pocket. I was expecting a typical knife, but it was something more unusual. The object was long and thin, made of red plastic and finished with a black end. I had no idea what the strange object was until He started clicking a little black switch on the side with his thumb. Slowly, a small blade with a very sharp angle began to protrude from the end.

Laughing with His friends, He proudly told of how He had swiped the craft knife from their design class. He followed it with a reference to the redundancy of His Yale key, stated with a theatricality which surprised me. His particular brand of banal malevolence was all His own, but it only really worked in the moment. In hindsight, His performance was laughably overblown.

The blade was fully in view, shining in the horrible blue light of the toilets. He started to conduct my movements with it, obeying every direction. I wondered what He was going to do. Slitting my face was too obvious. He couldn't risk that, otherwise He would be expelled. It probably didn't matter to Him a great deal, admittedly. He made swift cuts in the air towards my tie, and I noticed that the knife had already ripped several thin strands from it.

His followers grabbed my right arm and held it in an awkward position against my body, kept in place from behind by holding my hand close to my shoulder. They forcibly rolled up my coat and baggy jacket sleeve.

He almost drooled as He aimed the knife. He undid the button on my cuff and rolled the shirtsleeve down towards my elbow. Then He cut. The pain was awful, and I whimpered as blood dripped and stained the white shirtsleeve below. It wasn't a deep cut, but it was enough to scar.

Just as I felt the need to cry out, the voice from the earth returned. It possessed that gritty quality again, chewing rocks as it spoke. *Take the pain*, it said. The words lingered. I looked around, crying and asking why I should take such horror. The boys looked disturbed for a moment as I talked to the air, before pushing me to the floor. *Weirdo*.

He laughed and scampered off, followed by His little gang. I wondered what to do, how to stop the bleeding and hide it from the teacher of my next class, who would undoubtedly chastise me for being late. There was a roll of bumpy blue paper handtowels near one of the sinks, and I quickly stood up. The side of my leg was wet from being slumped on the floor. I stank.

It stung to touch the small cut, and bits of the towel were coming away and sticking to it. Luckily the shirt was only stained a little and had already done a good job of soaking up the spots of blood.

The paper towel turned from stern blue to a confusing purple as it halted the remaining flow. I slotted some underneath my shirtsleeve to use as a bandage and made do. I was incredibly late for my next class, but all I could think about were the gravelly words of support, the whispering marsh of the Mosslands.

Lessons afterwards dragged, not helped by the strong smell of my wet trousers, which several boys commented on. One boy asked the teacher whether I had wet myself and actually came over to check. Each second was punctuated by the stinging of my arm as I tried to write numbers. I raised the ire of Scratch & Sniff, who met me with his tactic of disappointed silence. He clearly noticed the smell after it was pointed out but said nothing, before he continued jostling his hands in his pants and sneaking smells of them in between talking. The blood had stopped running, but the pain was intense. It was akin to a zealous paper cut. My eyes filled with tears. No one noticed.

I stared blurrily onto the view of the marshland from the window high in the main building, taking pleasure in the rumbling of the motorway and its confident sway over the land. I would get there in the end, I thought, as I tried my best at the sums in front of me.

I would leave this place. At lunchtime, I would no longer play by the rules of the school, I thought. I would fade away under the motorway and no one would get me. It was worth the gamble to avoid all of this.

It had only taken two days of Him and His violent games to break me. I knew it would be dangerous venturing under the road – and not only because of the punishment if I was caught.

Dirt bikes could sometimes be heard zipping manically around underneath the concrete. People from the North End used the spot for drugs, lit fires there and set off fireworks. A local politician had even earmarked the space for a temporary container village to house the so-called Families from the North End; the families who seemed to spread violence throughout the area. All of this felt more welcoming than another lunchtime of His company.

The motorway was where I would escape. As I attempted to ignore the pain of my arm, I looked forward to the peace of the motorway over the Mosslands, optimistic for my disappearance.

◎

The boy was eager for the rock. Time was sterile and lifeless when away from it. When forced into school, he thought of little else but The Breck's stone walls. Everything seemed a waste of time in comparison to learning and mapping the routes to the top of the rock face.

After school, and sometimes before, he would venture to The Breck with one aim: to climb. The Breck had numerous high stone walls from its days as a quarry. It was a climber's paradise. He hated the fact that others threw their rubbish on its grass or set fire to it. The gorse made it even more beautiful in his eyes, and to be burned for no reason besides boredom was infuriating. He would take in the plant's scent when hanging from the rock face, its coconut odour drifting through the air when summer was slowly dying.

He loved the feel of his hands and fingers on the rough stone, exploring crevices. He felt he was taking a small part of it with him, the dust of each climb lingering on his clothes, much to his parents' dismay.

The feeling of the ground pulling the body down, understanding himself within the air, was addictive and alluring. He would climb Grannies Rock, a simple task for someone so quickly adept, just to consider himself on top of the world. The rock stood alone in the middle of the plateau. The view would glow from its pinnacle, filling his greedy eyes with joy.

Why weren't other people climbing? This was a question he would often consider, for there weren't many climbers then, even when he was developing the habit. It was long after the great boon of climbing interest many decades earlier when people would watch the footage of Mallory and Irvine, gasping in fear as captions of their deaths flashed up on the cinema screen in Birkenhead. Seeing two men, both from the peninsula, attempting such a feat was awe-inspiring, even thirty years on.

The boy had seen the film though he couldn't remember where. It had made his addiction worse. His climbing became more necessary in that final year of school. He wanted to stare from mountaintops; to travel to thin-air realms and unforgiving landscapes. For now, he would have to make do with The Breck's walls and Grannies Rock.

Occasionally, on the tall back walls, he would use a rope and even primitive hooks to aid and plan his climb. It was no longer a childish pastime but a question of skill and foresight, as serious as a game of chess played against stone.

Other children would watch him scale Grannies Rock, zipping up and down, his growing dexterity palpable in the way he read the rock's architecture. He knew the back wall in equal detail, such that he could draw it in his mind.

Although alone for the majority of his climbing, he always felt in company, always watched by a caring gaze. He could feel the skip in his step as he walked to The Breck, quickening his pace as he got closer to Breck Road.

After his body had accepted its limits and he was forced to rest, he would sit in the makeshift seat on top of Grannies Rock and look out. Welsh mountains rose in the distance, possible future conquests beckoning. He had scaled The Breck so many times that he soon dreamed of higher walls, bigger challenges. The light would fade and he would walk back, thinking of Grannies Rock and mountains and snow.

He felt the strength of his arms grow, his endurance increasing until there was little else left on The Breck that could battle efficiently against his skill. It was reverting to an easy game rather than the original challenge it had started as. He was merely using it to keep in shape until he was old enough to travel further, perhaps even in the footsteps of Mallory and Irvine.

The peace of The Breck was slowly disturbed by growing developments around it. New houses and retirement homes sprouted, overshadowing the dark trees. Climbing there was less and less pleasurable, more a necessity in order to retain the skills he had worked hard to gain. He wanted to join a climbing association and venture out from the peninsula, perhaps over The Dee into Wales.

The stone had been mapped by his hands through trial and error, until all its secrets, at least those in the physical world, had been found. He had heard ghost stories about The Breck and Grannies Rock, shrugging them off as children's tales. He knew the area too well to be fooled by superstition, to have his eyes diverted by falsities. Only the rock mattered.

He would deliberately block the view of the ground below from the roof of Grannies Rock, envisioning it to be much higher, imagining it closer to the clouds and beyond, rather than only a few feet high.

It was when autumn was threatening that the boy, now older, heard unusual questions. He himself had never considered such questions before, arising quickly within him. They would desist when at home, or even mere steps beyond The Breck. When within its rocky contours, questions, opportune questions even, could not help but form.

Was the rock itself asking such questions of him? Would life on the poor peninsula accommodate such a desire to climb? It was a childhood rite but only a select few had been allowed to continue that rite into adulthood, taking their imagination and naivety up higher mountain paths and walls of ice. The rest were left for the docks and factories. What were the chances that he, from somewhere as anonymous as this peninsula, would be allowed to continue?

An adventure like Mallory and Irvine's was what he wanted. He answered these initial questions quickly. His chances, in spite of his obvious skill, would be limited. But what if this could be bypassed with the same ease that he ascended Grannies Rock? The questions kept appearing. *What if this could be?*

The climbing of endless mountainsides, exploring the never-never. That would be the ideal scenario for the young man. He thought about climbing the hills in the distance as he stared out over the trees towards Wales. Even those mountainsides would do. Perhaps, with a good livelihood, he could explore them at weekends.

It would be just like those with their football on Sundays, down on the field by the marshes. But didn't he want more than that? A hobby was one thing, but would it fulfil his needs, his desires? What if there was only snow and rock and chasms of ice? What if the land was merely the hollow space carved from moaning glaciers, land that required many men just to enter its realms?

Imagine a landscape, he thought, brutal enough to freeze the souls from men, to slice and shred bodies, all from a minor miscalculation of movement or weather. Would those landscapes, those mountains, not be the ideal challenge? Far and away from the peninsula's plains, where the mountains were not ghosts on the horizon but the very heart of the land, all that the eye could behold. Was that not the future?

The images were heady and disorientating. He dreamed of standing on the peak of the world, far from The Breck and Grannies Rock. That was what he wanted.

What would he give for such a life?

He gazed out over the land, imagining crooked mountains rearing up. Perhaps he would give anything. He would give himself, his life even, just to see such heights. Anything that was his to give, just if he could climb, to fulfil his desire to see the world reduced to a miniature. He would give all for that prize.

And so, that is what he agreed.

◎

The changing world soon broke into the sealed life of the school. There was no possibility of keeping the real world away from the one locked inside those grey walls.

The walk home on the day He cut my arm was thankfully short, but I opted to take the steep hill rather than run through the allotments. My thinking was that there was little else He could do to me that could be worse.

The top of Wallacre Road turned onto the flat plateau of Breck Road. The marsh beyond was still visible in the distance. The motorway snaked beyond the horizon, and it looked especially welcoming when autumn finally set in. Mist would rise from the thick marshland in the coming weeks, rendering the concrete standing above it eerie, visible only by the occasional blurred glow of its neon lamps and the white and red lights of cars travelling in and out of its slip roads.

The sun had finally won out over the rain showers on that September day. Mornings felt heavy and muggy as the weather turned to autumn, but summer seemed to creep back during the afternoons.

I was walking with my friend from the previous school, who was still pestering me to trade the card he wanted. We were meandering along Breck Road when the news came through of a plane hitting a tower in New York. It sounded like a disaster film I had watched one Saturday afternoon with Mum, who had a crush on at least two of its actors. My friend, who never quite grew into himself, was listening to the developments on an orange plastic radio with headphones that resembled a hair band made of thin metal, distracting himself from his failed attempts to obtain the card he so wanted.

He said, half listening to the crackly updates, that a lot

of people had already died. I thought his listening to the news was incredibly grown up, far more grown up than anything I had particularly considered before. It gave him a more mature appearance than I had. It seemed unfair, not only because he was smaller than me, but also because he was weaker. Why wasn't he a chosen victim? I had automatically assumed from the insinuations the boys were making that their rage was roused because I wasn't a lad. But my friend was far more effeminate, especially in the way he walked. He wasn't a lad. He was a boy at most.

I considered then, as he repeated information about the plane that had smashed into the tower, that perhaps I should get some sort of portable radio to listen to news events such as this. Perhaps it would help me become an adult, though it was difficult to believe in adulthood when my trousers were still damp and my arm still sore from the cut.

My friend looked concerned as we walked back. As we came to the hill which led to my house, he said that he was confused. Another plane had apparently hit another tower, next to the first. He paid little attention to how I was holding my arm, which I gripped tightly around the strap of my bag. The blue paper towel was awkward and irritating underneath. I remember asking why there were two tall towers next to each other, far more surprised by that idea than the fact that a plane had managed to fly into each one.

My road was welcoming as I left my friend to walk on. I looked around before going down the hill. The thought of being followed by Him haunted me. What if the cut hadn't been enough to fulfil His need for violence? I had awful visions of Him learning where I lived and cornering me in the cul-de-sac. All possibilities raced through my mind with a horrible momentum.

Compared to the adjacent roads, all of which led down to the long marsh road on which the slowly sinking school lay, my road was different. The allotments thankfully separated the two roads.

Down the hill, the view showed part of the docklands, since derelict and occupied only by seabirds, behind which the marsh began again until it met with a smooth mound used as the local landfill site. I liked to imagine that underneath the greenery there was an endlessly busy world of cartons, cans, broken chairs, newspapers, smashed televisions, old fridges and the like. This may look nice, I thought, but everyone knows what is underneath, writhing.

At the end of the hill, the road stretched towards the iron railings of the allotments, behind which lay piles of compost, dead vegetables and general rubbish. In the middle of it, a large white pole always flew a St George's flag. The road itself was a dead end, marked by a pair of garages for the bigger houses at the end and a black felt square which separated their entrances, under which lived a colony of ants.

If He followed me to this place, I could not run. If I tried to get into the house, He would know where I lived. I could only hide, which would be utterly useless. I would have had to clamber the fence of the allotments, and run through its muddy paths back towards the small, barbed-wire fence and gate on the other side, opposite the neat playing field. I hoped that such a plan was never necessary.

There was a short palm tree planted in the front garden of our house. Around its base was an array of gravel which I soon daydreamed of using as a weapon. A handful of this dirt mixed with small, sharp stones could be thrown towards angry eyes in a hurry. I imagined the mouth of the marsh's voice filled with similar gravel, teeth biting down on its grit with a smile.

I slipped into the house, hoping again to hide the reality of the school before my parents returned, burying my unhappiness and my stained shirt. Mum's arrival was always denoted by raised voices on the mobile phone drawing nearer. Dad's was denoted by a knock at the back door to let him in after he had stored his bike in the shed.

My arm didn't look too bad with its small, singular red line. However, my shirt was stained with a few brown patches on the arm and a small rip in the material from the day before, when I had climbed over the allotment gate. There was no way to wash it quickly so I tore the whole shirt, carefully hiding it among some rubbish. It was placed with precision in the green, stale-smelling bin outside, hoping Mum and Dad wouldn't notice one missing shirt. My trousers needed washing, too.

Maybe if I crushed my eyes closed and forgot, the truth would crumble away. The cut on my arm, the nettle stings which still imprinted the backs of my legs, the bruises on my chest: they could simply dissolve. The motorway was to be my place of respite, I thought. Nothing so bad could happen to me there. I wouldn't have to daydream of escape for much longer.

◎

Wandering through childhood places also means wandering through the memories formed there. Streets feel smaller yet heavy as the past threatens to replay. The area around Mum's house felt brittle, as if parts of it might snap away.

I wanted to walk into the Mosslands and under the motorway, so I veered down a parallel hill that led to the marsh road. I felt the bulky Polaroid camera in my bag jolt into my back with each step.

Towards the end of the road, council houses began, as did the playing field where He had died. There was a separate path that curved behind the first houses on the road. Rather than face walking by the school buildings again, I followed this path. There was another allotment next to the field marked again with St George's flags and little black plastic bags hanging from every other fence post.

I was surprised, even after many visits to the motorway, just how close this path was to the busy road. The tarmac ran alongside a minor grassy incline, eventually leading to the raised part of the motorway.

The sound of vehicles was overwhelming. I had very few memories of approaching the area from this side, but either way, it was always noisy. I had usually visited from the side of the school. This side was green in part, though not that shimmering emerald that radiated by the railway lines and the marsh beyond; staining the air jade. Weeds sprouted from the ground like fingers, soon to reveal the palms of an unimaginable pair of hands. It was a softer green by this path, created by simple weeds and shrubs growing through patches of roadside rubbish.

The field opened out to the right, and I was met with the sight of my old school. It loomed out of the ground, still possessing the power to intimidate. I could not face down the field, remembering the police tape and the grainy black-and-white images printed in local newspapers when His body was found. The furore surrounded the area for only a few days before it died down. It became just another sad story from the peninsula. It had contaminated the field in my thoughts, and all I could see when looking at it were visions of His body smeared over the grass, as if a large butter knife had spread it over the ground until nothing was left but a mangle of flesh and soil.

I walked on, as I knew a train would soon be passing and I wanted to experience the sound under the motorway. Like the smaller bridge on School Lane, the sound beneath it was shattering. The noise was already incredible as the tarmac curved under the grey structure. Along with the exhale of cars, I could hear the quiet murmur of boys confined within the walls of the classrooms over the way.

Sunlight was taken by the concrete and all manner of images floated back from memory. My first visit here was not long after He cut my arm. There was a sense of disappearance that occurred immediately when sat against one of the road's concrete plinths as its vibrations travelled through the spine. I had spoken at length in shadow-tongue to the voice from the marshland. It all came back.

Ahead was the rustling greenery on the other side of the train tracks. Behind the high metal fence which protected the railway, all that existed to the north was the cavern underneath the road. It shrank into a vanishing point, though I knew it couldn't continue indefinitely. Graffiti was scrawled everywhere. Symbols constantly renewed themselves and vied for space on the skin of the road.

The path wound its way into the buzzing marshland. Then, around a sharp corner, there was a small, shining footbridge with overhanging mesh extending in several directions, over a patch of water to the left and railway tracks to the right.

I could see the motorway perfectly on the other side. A desire path led into its shadows. Plant life was virulent and successfully hid a hardware store whose warehouse stood defiantly behind the thickest of the vegetation, sinking like all of the buildings there.

I stood transfixed for a moment in the sun's heat, before feeling too hot and walking into the shade of the road. It felt unusually pleasant to be back and I allowed memories to resurface. The land was alive, and although I felt the voice from the ground would not return, the air trembled with life all the same.

The area under the motorway was laid with concrete and half-finished roads. In between them sprouted an array of fauna and debris. The thick concrete support pillars of the road above marked out the shape of the space, directing the eyes to a point at which the road eventually vanished. Each metal carriageway had gaps which revealed the various signs of the motorway and the glint of passing vehicles above. The space seemed to go on forever when following the direction of the road.

I fumbled in my bag for the Polaroid camera. I wanted to angle the photo perfectly, to capture the point when the marsh began and the road ended, or vice versa. I wanted the fragment of sky there, too. The whole place needed locking away in the Polaroid.

The camera flashed, and out crawled a blank photograph from its mouth. Something stopped me from going further, perhaps the realisation that it was only my first day back and I didn't want to overwhelm myself. Memories can bloat the body and mind, like a rich meal for the soul.

I stared at this living view for a while. It provided an opportunity to make sure the image developed properly and clearly. There were obviously no seats on the path, as it wasn't an official place. The ground was dry from the unforgiving sunlight, so I sat cross-legged, observing the view.

Cars zipped by without a second thought for what was below. Only a destination was important. I must have seemed absurd to anyone who saw me, hiding like a schoolboy in the grass, playing a game far beyond my years.

I noticed the under-layer of rubbish once at ground level.

The plants had happily grown over it. The metallic carcass of something burned into a skeletal sculpture sat further under the road. The area still had the ability to diminish personal problems, rendering them equal to the debris all around. It soaked those troubles up and used them for its own purposes.

The colours of the photograph developed quickly, a miniature of the motorway forming in the palm of my hand. My worry over the end of the school day soon grew again. Time spent in the grass was drained of enjoyment as pleasure receded into nervousness. I had half an hour before the boys were due to be released. Yet I really had little to worry about. This was a land, after all, that protected its lonely sons.

# 2

The falling towers flooded the lives of adults. School was equally submerged under rolling news, the events spoken about obsessively by teachers and pupils alike. Every night that week, once home from a day of work, my parents sat mesmerised in horror by the developments. Coverage of the planes crashing took over their lives. It became hard to imagine a time when images of planes smashing into buildings wasn't normal.

Dad was particularly drawn to it, noting every developing detail and piece of information, though his mind was seemingly occupied with other things. He sat in his jeans and a Hawkwind T-shirt after work, watching the news carefully. His face was sharpened by the exercise he constantly took, looking much younger than he really was. I would gradually inherit his long nose, bright eyes and high hairline, but sadly not his persistent youthful appearance. He aged at a slower rate than most.

I noticed a change in the way Dad smiled. Though he still smiled regularly, something I found reassuring, the moment of it leaving his face was more obvious. Perhaps it was a considered gesture for his son in the new, more dangerous world we had woken up in. His eyes, I noticed with worry, stopped smiling before his mouth, the two in disjuncture.

Mum was little changed, however. The events of that week allowed her various worries to find a new, more corporeal fixture, but that was all. Her face was its usual warm, confident self even when footage of the atrocity was reflected in her blue eyes. The corners of her eyelids creased behind her wiry glasses when she smiled at me as she sat in the grey suit she wore to work. It was she who would eventually turn the channel over to something lighter and break the news cycle, determined to replace the planes with shows about interior design.

I could not tell them about how those first few days at the school were developing. I felt my body language shift that week. I can't recall in detail what happened in the days that followed His attack with the knife, other than a repetition of name calling and rough pushes and shoves. Those days were filled with towers falling and planes crashing more than anything else.

French was still a particularly awful lesson, as the teacher decided to perform a mock apology during each register every time he pronounced my surname. Darting around the yard at break failed to protect me completely either, though I avoided further physical torment of the sort which had inducted me into life at the school.

The sky looked unusual in the days that followed. When not blackened by rain clouds and visiting showers turning the yard into a small lake, the blue was stingingly clear. All planes had been grounded, and where jet streams had previously bisected the air, now an endless autumn blue beamed. It was strange how clear the sky was without planes. The blue was so vivid that I hoped it would gush down and drown us all. In my fantasies, the yard was drowned in sky-wet mud and returned to the damp marshland beyond.

Finding sanctuary under the motorway was postponed again as it rained sporadically that week, forcing us indoors at break times. I was worried I would cry; a scenario which, by the unwritten laws of the school, would mean utter oblivion.

Sat at a table indoors, a boy I didn't know jumped and thrust his hands on my head. Salt had been gathered from several tiny blue sachets made of thin paper and poured into my tatty hair. He even made a pun about how I had been 'a-salted'. I was surprised at how little I was bothered by this humiliating action, nor by the carton of milk – flattened and thinned of its outer cardboard, allowing it to burst on the slightest impact – that would be thrown at my back during the morning break on Friday.

Even as I ran my hands through my hair and felt the gritty texture of the salt, or started to smell the milk turning stale on my blazer jacket before lunch, all I could think of was how amateur these attempts were compared to His efforts. Their bullying was inconsequential compared to the bruises on my chest or the thin cut on my arm.

The atmosphere in the school receded into something more banal but more dangerous. Only a day after the attack on the towers, graffiti soon appeared like cave paintings on tables and doors, scratched into the wood. The words expressed violence towards Muslims, calling for them to be killed and kicked out of the country. I considered the possibility that it could have been Him, cutting into the wood and doors with the same knife He had used to slice my arm.

Aside from glaring with glee at the back of my head during another of our shared French lessons, He and His lads had merely conducted others to work me over rather than build upon the violence of those first days. I had a feeling, later proved right, that there was a limit in regards to His violence. Only a certain amount a week was tolerated, as it meant less chance of getting into trouble, and because it actually took effort on their part. The quota had been met for that week, so He sat back and happily watched the virus of His ideas spread to others.

I felt rusted and old inside, creaking around between each lesson. It reminded me of a story Granddad once told me about the dockers in Birkenhead. He worked on the ships and often brought a collection of characters home each week, much to the frustration of my nan. She came home one night to a group of Danish sailors and a donkey in the garden. After the shipping and docking jobs were lost in the 1980s, the sadness of the men Granddad worked with was so great that it began to crumble their skin. Many would eventually jump to the bottom of the

West Float basin or Alfred Dock, apparently rusted like anchors. They called their sadness Dread Iron.

It was during the lunch break on Friday that I finally escaped under the motorway. Looking back years later, when old enough to be allowed to go home every lunch break, the thought of having to hide under a motorway seemed absurd.

As the bell rang, the feeling of fear rose again. I had only a short amount of time to make my escape, still smelling of stale milk. If anyone caught sight of me slipping out the front gate, it would have meant trouble. A teacher could have reprimanded me, a pupil could have informed on me or, worse still, informed Him. Yet the day was with me. Time froze as I noticed the unusual pull with which my steps were guided from the edge of the yard and through the unguarded main gate.

A path, only recently laid, ran along the side of the field all the way to the edge of the marsh and the giant hogweed surrounding a patch of rail-side water. It then snaked round and went under the motorway. Many older boys were on the field already, sitting on carefully placed bags to avoid the damp ground, or playing football with a variety of objects, one large game revolving around a plastic bottle filled with water.

I felt more secure here, if only because I could blend in. I concealed my sleeves deep inside my pockets, hiding the missing sewn-on band which denoted being allowed out of school during breaks. I edged my way closer to what I felt was a divide on the playing field where it inclined as it approached the marsh. The rise made sports impossible there, so no boys were nearby. This was the end of the field and the most dangerous point of the journey, where I was most likely to be seen.

A train rumbled along the track, its roar getting closer and rendering the land a void until it had gone. This was my chance. As the train sped by, I turned from my watchful position overlooking the school and ran full pelt alongside, following the noise until the environment turned into the motorway.

The train left me alone at the end of the path as I panted for breath. I was pleased. It felt like a return home.

Plants grew wildly all around, even with autumn approaching. They leaned towards what little light filtered through the gaps in the road above. In between the stems of the various scrub, rubbish banded together, forming a layer that glimmered when the rays travelled under the road.

I crossed the bridge quickly, still worried that my presence on that part of the path could cast a silhouette easily seen from somewhere in the school. Underneath the bridge were the railway tracks. One disused line slipped under the brown water of a pond, where a pair of swans floated through the reeds. I could not see the main path which led under the motorway, only brown mud walked into the ground by other wanderers of the marsh.

The route leading further into the marsh itself was overgrown, the reeds and plants creating an overhanging walkway. I took the path on the right leading to the motorway. I wanted its noise, its abandonment, and the unnamed desire which grew within due to the spirit of the soil. This was where it wanted me to go, for my own safety.

Underfoot, there was a Left Turn Only arrow directed pointlessly to a smattering of concrete and abandoned roadways. But the roads led to nowhere, marked further only by minor bits of rubble, a derelict fence, rusted drinks cans, plastic bags, a needle and some building debris. The motorway cavern stretched far beyond, pausing only to make way for a roundabout some way ahead.

I walked under the road, feeling instantly safe. Berries were growing on some of the plants, sprouting poisonous colours which glowed between the vast green and yellow of the reeds. A leather sofa sat right in the centre of the concrete plain, fly-tipped and left to rot. It felt like it appeared from nowhere. I couldn't remember seeing it when first looking around. Its once white leather had been rendered a dark, dirty cream by pollution and dust. I sat down on its torn fabric, the view hypnotic with its perfect symmetry of road and land. I sat eating my lunch in peace, alone except for the growling cars and the occasional bird.

Contrary to how the area had been portrayed by adults, it was an array of colour and life. The concrete had neon graffiti all over it, in competition with nuclear ragwort, which grew in confident patches. My worries simmered to a manageable level as I sat on the sofa, wondering why other boys never came here. Perhaps they did, but I never saw them.

This was my space, I felt. Being under the motorway

and finding happiness and solace, I wondered what other spaces I had neglected; places supposed to be dangerous and dirty but which, in my new desperate state, could potentially mean everything.

I lost track of time, minutes ticking away as each new aspect was noticed, like a living film that provided no narrative other than what was passing by. I forgot about the bullying, the bruises and the other injuries incurred in the school. The only thing that mattered was the comfort of this space which had welcomed me into its arms and cared for me like a third parent.

From a distance, I heard the wailing bell of the school, still so loud even from far away. The feeling that arrived with the sound was like grief.

One of my lessons was with Him in the afternoon, yet another French lesson, followed by a Science lesson, thankfully without Him. I expected the usual scene with the French teacher during the register. At first, the thought was unbearable. Yet I felt stronger knowing that this place was here. My body moved slowly and resisted leaving the space. Tears filled my eyes, and this time I let them flow. They were met by the voice.

I wish I could recall what it said. Its scratching nature collapses in my memory every time I try to remember. I know it guided me gently back to the pathway as my tears subsided.

I snuck back in with the last boys walking into the building via the side gate, and looked towards the motorway with affection and relief. Even His presence failed to move me in French. He might as well have glared at me through reeds and concrete.

This was the end of the first week at the school in the Mosslands.

◉

I was thinking about Grannies Rock, the large stone that stands in the heart of The Breck. The large slab of rock had occupied my mind ever since I first planned my trip home. Even more than the motorway, the rock exerted an unusual pull.

I told people in London about Grannies Rock whenever I could. It gave people the false impression that I grew up somewhere like Avebury or Glastonbury. It was a bastard cousin of those menhirs, shamed and abandoned compared to those looked after by the National Trust and English Heritage. The Breck has no gift shop.

Mum arrived back from work that first night of my return, still tussling with the unhappiness of the same tough job she had been working since I was a child. Her face lit up on seeing me, in spite of shouting at a colleague on her phone at the same time. Some of her security men had been caught thieving from a house in Liverpool.

It had been several months since we had last seen each other. As always when meeting her, there was sadness in her eyes, born of the fact that our sense of home had faded. Dad was now living elsewhere and I was living far away in London.

We reflected each other's smiles that evening like distant beacons. The late summer sun shone through the net curtains, creating slow-moving shapes coloured with differing shades of beige. I had always loved the designs created by the sun on this wallpaper. It happily reminded me of being allowed days off from school when I was ill.

Mum asked how I was, worried as always about life in London. She quickly settled herself on the couch after a few more questions about living in the capital, something I was just coping with financially. She and her partner, still relatively new in the household, were preparing for the move. The atmosphere became awkward as we discussed it, knowing how much I really wanted her to stay on Merseyside. I would miss it more than I could tell.

I knew then that it was the right time to visit The Breck. The area would need more than one visit, such was the pleasure of its grassy pastures; a messy patch of land which I hoped would never be subjected to tidiness.

I left the pair to watch the news, picking up my camera from my room, though not before Mum asked in worry about my walking on The Breck at such a time. I wondered what her partner thought of her strange son, wandering skittishly in and out of the house with an old Polaroid camera.

At the top of my hill, The Breck loomed. Its trees leaned ominously over the road. The sunlight receded behind clouds and the area was darker than I had anticipated. But the warm rays returned intermittently, casting shadows across the busy road as if it was its own private canvas.

I crossed over to the old schoolhouse, a small brick

building so covered with moss that it looked as wooden as the trees threatening to engulf it. There was something wrong, however, and my unease grew. Then I noticed what was causing it. A large white flagpole that protruded from a stone staircase leading to nowhere had been repainted. A bright flag flew at the top, suggesting the formation of a local preservation group. A new blue plaque sat on the wall, celebrating the history of climbing on The Breck thanks to a famous mountain climber. This climber, the plaque said, had made use of the large sandstone walls when younger, his skills honed there before the inevitable move away.

The area *had* been tidied up.

I looked up more about the climber later on, finding out that he had been the first British man to ascend K2, though he was killed on the descent, left by the others in the hope they would be spared a slow death from the storm that had dramatically pummelled the mountainside. It felt an infinitely long way from The Breck, the only mountains in view being those of North Wales in the distance.

I climbed the long steps into its moody forest, unsure of where I really was. I wondered what the voice, which had spoken so powerfully within me in those weeks after the terrible start at school, thought of such renovation.

The grass had been mown. The dips created naturally from past quarrying of the area had provided little resistance, now possessing a neat buzz-cut of yellowing green. The sunlight was free to beam down, drying out much of the plant life in those last weeks of summer. And then there was Grannies Rock itself, the sandstone monolith that had stood on The Breck for as long as anyone could remember.

Thankfully, it was still awkward and ugly. I had expected it to have grown smaller, but it was still monumental. The vivid spray-paint that had marked its uneven skin had been sanded away, leaving only the most ambitious of carved names faintly legible on the stone.

Grannies Rock had always resembled a shrunken, stubby mountain. Its crags had the sort of detail that resembled an old mountainside viewed from afar, detail which vanished back into the rock on closer inspection. The top of the rock was still unusually flat. I remembered how some believed it to be one of the supports for the mining cranes used to drag the sandstone out of the landscape, the same material laid down to form the coastal road further along the peninsula.

I used to imagine large tendrils growing under the earth, snaking all of the way down the hillside to the marshland under the motorway; as if the stone was a vast node, a connecting point where the long, thin fingers of the marshland's spirit secretly met and formed an intelligence of sorts. It was the consciousness of the marshland and the voice that spoke to me.

I used to be far more imaginative when I was a child. Then I went to university.

The branches overhead looked black and the tree creaked ominously. I let my hand map the face of the rock, its rough texture comforting as my fingers found a hole large enough to act as a handhold. I levered my weight up, hanging there by my fingers, swinging from side to side like a door on its hinges. But the memory of why I had stopped climbing the rock returned quickly.

Climbing Grannies Rock had once been a regular activity, a natural occurrence for somewhere with so little else to do. Hanging off its craggy face and sitting around The Breck was exciting. I still recall my parents finding out what we – myself and some kids from my road – were doing, the reason why we couldn't be seen from the window in front of where we normally played the day they discovered our trespass. When they had checked the road, not a child was in sight.

The Breck was alluring, being a large space with trees to climb and stones to throw. The problem, according to my parents, was not simply the dirty, dangerous nature of the place, but the road below it which was always busy with cars. We were not supposed to go to The Breck, never mind climb Grannies Rock.

Sometimes we fell onto the soft ground and it seemed to catch our small bodies like a caring pair of hands. Even the swaying trees could not block the view from the top of Grannies Rock, the skyline threatening to swing and knock us from the rocky pedestal, its overwhelming colour confronting our tiny eyes. But these pleasures were taken away by a story of such power that, even then on The Breck as an adult remembering it, I had slowly stopped my half-climb of Grannies Rock and stood back with respect.

Mum had taken me to one side, after seeing us sneakily return thanks to a chance glance from my bedroom window. I remember the chair she sat me on, how big it seemed and how unusually formal the scenario felt. She did not want me to go to The Breck any more. It was dangerous, and if something happened to me, they wouldn't know until it was too late. I can see how carefree my response was to this plea, still retaining the firm belief in my own invincibility that most children carry with them.

Seeing that I wasn't really listening, she told me the story of a boy. When Mum had heard the story, she was roughly the same age as I was then. I could not picture Mum being my own age. It seemed an absolute impossibility.

She could not remember the boy's name, but it was beside the point. This boy had climbed Grannies Rock too, in the 1970s, and as a teenager he had impressed the younger children with his skill in climbing the stone. He became possessive of it in the time of Mum's childhood and eventually bullied anyone he found nearby. The stone was his alone.

The boy had died.

I was surprised she was telling me such a dark story. She had always been incredibly wary of things that could stop me from sleeping, being far too gentle for my own good. Even certain episodes of my beloved science-fiction show could only be viewed when a parent was present, especially one with terrifying alien plants that turned people green. But she was telling me this story deliberately to scare. This was an exception. I needed to be scared.

The boy had died because he was not very well, apparently, and had decided to take his own life. He had gathered some rope which he took to The Breck at night. He had climbed the rock, and flung the rope around the nearby tree, one that still was creaking in the wind as I recalled the story. The boy hanged himself and was found the following day.

Mum was insistent that my school, when Dad was a pupil there, had warned pupils away from going to The Breck due to this. I found the story unnerving, but was uncertain why it was being told to me. Mum perhaps thought a macabre death would quell my curiosity regarding The Breck, but it did the opposite. It would be like climbing a large gravestone, a thought which gave me an excited, eerie chill. But this was not the end of the story.

Mum then told me about sightings of the boy since his death.

On certain nights, a body could supposedly be seen swaying from the tree. One boy had felt dangling legs brush against him when he was climbing the rock. Most threatening of all, born of the boy's obsession with the stone, his unsettled spirit was still angered by anyone else climbing it. If I were to climb the rock, then his hanging body would appear and he would scream at the climber to get down. He would yell and thrash about at the end of the rope like a snared animal.

I remember still how I shivered at her words. The thought of a boy screaming from the top of the rock was too much to bear. It inverted all my unreal daydreams about the living and the dead.

How would such a scream sound? What would his rotten, crumbling mouth have looked like, screaming at me to get off Grannies Rock? My imagination went wild. I could

see loose teeth falling on me, leathery strands of skin and
bones raining down as he screamed and fell apart, writhing
about at the end of the rope. The thought still chills me.

I wandered away from the rock. The sun was out
again, and I worried that, due to the camera's deficiency
in bright light, the rock would evade my capture. It was a
mischievous stone.

I was not used to the workings of the Polaroid camera
either, being much more comfortable with a simple 35mm.
I had borrowed it from my friend Ellen. She was a talented
fashion photographer who embodied the city we lived in and
made beautiful, esoteric work shown all over the capital. I
noticed the various stickers she had stuck to the grey plastic
outer casing of the camera. It made me miss London a little,
but I put the feeling aside as I set up the shot of Grannies Rock.

The little light on the camera flashed green and I pressed
the large rubbery button to turn the flash off. The sun was
providing too much light already. I leaned back gently
against another rise of smoothly worn sandstone, letting
the camera mechanism work away. Its organs churned
until, with a tired sigh, it printed out the likeness.

Despite my lingering thoughts of the hanging boy, I
didn't want to go back to Mum's house yet. I decided to
enjoy the sunny pasture instead, as the evening lazily drew
in. Like my childhood self, I sat perched on the miniature
stone seat looking towards Grannies Rock, daring the
hanging boy to show himself. I tried again to remember
details of the voice from the soil, what it had said, how I
had followed its instructions. But it was still beyond me.

The photo darkened before a heavy yellowish light entered. I imagined a scenario from a film I had seen where a photographer accidentally captured the strange anomalies floating around those soon to be murdered by a devilish curse. The method of death would appear through abstract shapes and marks on his photos, impaling one man, decapitating another. Perhaps something cursed would arise from my photograph.

Grannies Rock finally appeared on the Polaroid. For a fraction of a moment, I thought I saw a darkened object hanging behind it. But, checking the trees around the rock with my own eyes, the image morphed quickly into the bright light of the late summer evening and disappeared.

There was nothing there now but stone and memories.

◎

My insect understanding of the world continued as life at school developed its patterns and rhythms. I scuttled away at every opportunity. Though the motorway shielded me from lunchtime attacks, I could not escape so easily during the morning breaks.

For those fifteen minutes I had to fend for myself, keeping on the move. After only a week, the few boys I could previously rely on for friendship had learned of my dangerous baggage. They knew that He and His small gang had developed a sort of understanding with me, some even believing that I had a demented friendship with Him. I was avoided, left to roam.

He found me almost instantly the following Monday break, dragging me behind the woodwork block without much trouble before the usual beating. I was already exhausted and battered from the morning's Games, which He had bunked yet again by not bringing any kit. I felt the dried mud fall with each punch and kick.

There was a commotion in the yard that morning. A porn magazine had been smuggled in. Unusually, it had been torn to shreds within minutes. Stray fragments of flesh were found for days afterwards. The images of women's bodies had been so confusing for some, producing a mixture of attraction and disgust, that the only reaction left had been to tear them apart. The odd teacher on duty could be seen sneakily capturing bits under their shoes and stealing glances down in between keeping an eye on the boys.

While this was happening, He asked where I went at lunchtime last week, clearly noticing my disappearance. I did not tell Him. My neck was strangled with my tie as an interrogation, but I would never tell Him about the motorway. The marsh provided a mental block to His taunts, effective to such an alarming degree that even His followers shared nervous glances when their startling violence got them nowhere.

I would retreat more and more to the motorway that week, sneaking out at lunchtime with such regularity that I was soon surprised by how easy it seemed. Teachers were always handily drawn away by minor diversions: a group of boys dangerously throwing stones at the windows of passing trains, fights breaking out at the precise moment when I needed a clear run to the path, or a football flying over a fence resulting in an outcry for the teacher on duty to go and get it.

On Thursday, something finally broke the routine. He had misjudged His angle behind me in the morning break, trying to push me into a doorway near the lunch hall. It was a risky strategy, as it provided little cover from the eyes of others. He did it anyway.

Having found me loitering, He blocked me within the small frame of the door and applied various pushes and punches. Adrenaline left my hands frozen to the point where it felt as if I was crushing the bones of my fingers in my own grip. A teacher spied what was happening and dashed over heroically. The look of utter fatigue on his face was clear as he broke up the gathering, pushing boys apart and trying to understand what was going on. Nerves froze my mouth tight shut.

I thought of the marsh, wandering within it in my mind and imagining giant hogweed turning His skin to bloated yellow balloons. I imagined the pain the marsh nettles would cause to His body, bound tightly around Him like poisonous rope. I thought of luring Him under the motorway and beating His head with slabs of broken concrete, crushing Him into the dirty tarmac. I could see the grit and dirt from the road mixing with his demolished skull, forming a dark red paste.

I would kill Him.

I let the teacher direct me away from the boys, one hand heavy on my shoulder. The morning break ended and I felt my chest deflate with relief, to the point where I could barely walk to my Science lesson. Nothing more was made of the incident, as if such violence was expected, normal.

I hated Science as the windows in the laboratories were all impossible to look out of properly. Nothing of the motorway or the marsh could be seen. Even imagination could not alleviate the feeling of being closed in. I soon found a temporary solution to this problem thanks to my parents.

At the weekend, we travelled for a day out, rumbling for miles along never-ending roads until the land around us sprouted mounds and green hills, eventually evolving into small mountains. We were heading to Wales, and I lapped up the countryside. The bruises on my arm and the ache that accompanied them faded with the fresh air.

I liked our destination, an unusual rocky park called Loggerheads. Dark trees followed its incline all the way up to a precipice that hung high over the car park. It was busy, filled with people dispersing rapidly into the paths and forest around.

As we followed the river running along the pathway into the woods, Mum, dressed in warm clothing including a yellow woolly hat, asked how my first two weeks of school had been. I did a good job of lying, making up boring details to move the conversation on. Lists of friends, cards swapped at break time, the best teachers like the Art teacher who played us The Beatles, the worst teachers like Scratch & Sniff, how the children I had known from the previous school had settled in, and all manner of other details.

Dad then distracted us by pointing out a dipper on the river. He let us look through the binoculars he always carried on days out. He was incredibly excited, loudly calling the bird's name out. I watched the little bird bob up and down on a rock, the white patch of its body almost touching the gushing water, threatening to sweep it away. It flew further down the river in search of food, so we moved on.

The horror of school receded while walking. Soon we made it to the top of the precipice, which looked out over the landscape. Mum said we were near a place called World's End, a name which fired my imagination, as if the only thing left there would be the horizon.

Dad pulled out a new digital camera, surprising in how compact it was. We were able to see photographs instantly.

It felt like magic. He had saved up to buy it and couldn't contain his anticipation. The small silver box bore a tiny screen to display the photograph once it was taken. It made photography seem fleeting. I would grow to hate it as an adult, to the point where I would only use older cameras out of a sort of analogue spite. At the time, however, seeing pixelated photos instantly was thrilling.

Spellbound by the view from the ridge, I asked Dad to photograph it for me. I wondered if he would print off a copy on his battered printer once home, a big ask as the printer was only for printing special documents beyond my understanding. He agreed, and once we were home, he uploaded the photographs to the computer.

The cold air of Loggerheads travelled through the screen as the moody mixture of grey and green photos appeared one by one. He highlighted one particular photograph, the one I said I liked the most. He formatted it before loading the printer with paper and switching it on. The image slowly came into existence, the printer scratching it out line by line. The Welsh landscape appeared blurry on the page but I was still excited at having it there in my hands. Dad gifted it to me with a smile.

I wandered off in awe of the image. Soon I had more ideas about what to do with it. It was not an image to go on my wall. I didn't need one, considering the view of The Breck out of the window. I searched for a pair of scissors, cutting around the image until it was no longer a small corner on a large white canvas. It was now pocket-sized, a miniature landscape. It may not have been the motorway, but it would do. Perhaps I could ask Dad to take one of the marsh for me too in the coming weeks. I intended to keep this photograph in my blazer pocket, for those moments I found myself in the rooms with bad views out of the window. I could fall into it and away from school for a time.

The picture proved its worth the following week, staring at it during the tedium of the lessons. It even removed the ache of being battered in Games once more. The mini landscape quickly lost its colours and crinkled, the shades warping into strange blotches of white, pink and green.

I disliked the order of lessons in Week A, as it was called in our planner, more than Week B – it had more Science classes and more classes with Him. In Science again, aching from His kicks and punches, I disappeared into the image and onto the precipice of Loggerheads, sneaking glances whenever I could. Much later, at the end of the term, my report discussed my daydreaming, labelling me as an idler who spent too much time drifting out of the lessons.

Later in the week, after miraculously avoiding the boys at morning breaks for a few days on the run, a beating was owed. They finally cornered me and went through my pockets, finding the printed landscape. I felt an overwhelming need to cry out. He took the printed landscape, along with my school planner.

Slowly and gleefully, He tore both things up before my eyes, covering me in fragments of the landscape, confetti of trees and rock and daydreams. It was a painful moment and my despair shone through, much to His delight. He was goading me into crying, or worse, trying to fight back.

I watched as the torn rock floated down onto the yard, horrified. I had quickly grown to rely on it. The bell rang but I could not move. Tearing up my miniature landscape was more powerful than whipping my legs with nettle stems or cutting my arm with a craft knife. The boys ran off, but He lingered to savour my upset as I bent down to try and pick up the pieces. They were already soggy on the damp tarmac.

The next lesson was Art. The teacher put on a CD of Jimi Hendrix and asked us to spend the rest of the lesson drawing or painting a picture portraying a place that was important to us. He started to draw stylised images of New York to the soundtrack of 'Crosstown Traffic'. I felt the marsh had taken control of the teacher and had forced him to give me the opportunity to mourn my destroyed landscape.

I thought of painting the motorway or its surrounding marsh, but worried that evidence of knowing the area in detail would raise questions. Instead, I opted to recreate the photograph that had been torn up.

Most of the others painted football stadiums and pitches from different angles: the pitch, the seats and the buildings seen in Anfield, Everton and Tranmere. As I gathered the paint and sketched what I could remember from the photograph, my hands left my control. I watered down the thick blue and black poster paint, to the point where it was almost watercolour, so that the sky would be filled with Welsh darkness.

I sketched the hill with pencil and left it as it was, looking charred, before throwing on green paint mixed to various shades, and then the trees, which had their bark further scratched onto them like they were made of stone.

The painting achieved its effect with such alarming speed that even the teacher was surprised as he walked around and checked on our progress. He watched over my shoulder as I rubbed at the ground, solid like the hill where I had stood the previous weekend. I was in a trance, listening as a voice directed my actions, but with words I could not understand.

It was the only painting I was ever happy with. The image showed a moody place. It lacked the school's stupidity of bricks, its cackling weeds and the fear that permeated every room like fog.

The bell rang annoyingly, signifying that the double period was over. I didn't want to leave the landscape behind, wishing I could pocket it and use it like the printed photograph. But it was too big and still wet. I imagined the trees smearing themselves into blurs on the inside of my bag, so I left it on the pile, looking longingly towards it before leaving.

The painting had distracted me from my usual plan of escape. Luckily, Art was always in that strange block built into the older boys' yard, so I had less distance to cover. I restrained my natural desire to run, wondering where He could be. I hoped He was stuck in the other yard, picking on someone else.

The motorway exerted its pull. It carried me through the gate next to the field, which the older boys were walking through, ready to muddy themselves once again in games of football on the damp grass. I could feel the marsh breathing by my side, its clumps of distant hogweed murmuring approval as I made my way under the harsh concrete, over the railway and down into the heart of the land.

I had fallen into the habit of talking to the marsh, aiming words under the motorway but firm in the belief that they were heard. Sometimes the marsh replied, but I could never remember what was said. I told the marsh about my torn photograph, how the bullies were going to be there forever. I told the marsh about Him again. It was my usual topic of conversation, the reason I was there to talk at all.

Tears formed as I recounted what had happened to the photograph. It had meant so much to me, just to be able to escape the school for a few seconds. I wished Him harm. The whole of school life was painfully dragging me out of childhood. How was I to deal with it all?

The breeze flittered around the concrete as I sat cross-legged in the middle of the labyrinth, sometimes pausing in my outpouring of problems to read the latest graffiti and eat my lunch. The voice encircled me before leaving. Then I was alone.

The bell sounded in the distance and my heart dropped. I made to leave with care. Returning from the motorway without being seen was just as important as entering.

I said my farewell to the marsh, affectionately patting one of the large concrete pillars that held up the road. Before I left, the breeze caught up with me, blowing all manner of rubbish, twigs and leaves in its wake, a ragged ghost of debris. It almost looked like a man.

The voice of the marsh had parting words for me. I long to remember them in full, but they always slip away. I do remember one thing the gravelly voice said as I stood on the metal bridge. In between the cars roaring and the swaying of the vegetation, the voice clearly and calmly spoke with confidence two very distinct words.

*The Breck.*

I initially rushed home after school at the end of the week. Yet, I wanted to stay outside when I finally reached the top of my road. I needed to wander. My legs dawdled when walking past the trees of The Breck.

It was clear that He was unlikely to trouble me after hours, unless it was some prearranged grab close to the school buildings. Already prepared for such an outcome, I varied my exit from the school every day, dodging back and forth between buildings until I felt sure I was able to make the first few roads safely.

I felt safer walking the streets nearer my home,

shadowed by the trees of The Breck. Even then, the littered pasture was an ominous place. I could never shake the stories of the hanging boy, but after listening to the voice in the Mosslands, The Breck seemed more welcoming than it ever had before. Its trees, rather than having hanging, screaming bodies hidden within them, hinted at sanctuary.

The Breck was quiet. The busy traffic of the road was firmly silenced. It was a Friday, so the other boys from school, and the girls from their nearby equivalent, had dissipated quickly, happy that another week was over.

I quickly looked around as I stood at the bottom of the strange steps that led through the forest. I was alone as I followed the dark green path. It was several years since I had been there, but the place had not changed. Grannies Rock appeared to pull the ground towards it, as if the land was a carpet and the rock had been placed on top of a concealed hole; slowly sinking, dragging everything closer. The leaves were already off the trees, being early autumn, and a view could be seen of the motorway, the business park and the land beyond.

The area still seemed green, even if it was of an olive colour. Vegetation created an organic shimmer in the air. I wasn't going to climb Grannies Rock, still superstitious about the hanging boy, but I did want to see it.

The grass was damp, making my shoes gleam, green blades sticking to them with each step. I could barely bring myself to even touch the stone, standing before the rock politely as if in the presence of an elder who required respect.

A question formed in my mind, as if from nowhere.

What did I really want, more than anything in the whole world? The question carried great importance as I stood in front of Grannies Rock, yet seemed to be asked in a voice that wasn't my own.

I leaned with my back against the rock, forgetting my fear of touching it. Questions surged through me.

What did I want?

I thought of material things at first, wishing my parents didn't have to work so they could be happy. Perhaps I could reverse the falling of the towers in America and save all those people, rewinding the footage of the towers crumbling into a fog of fire and dust.

I ran my finger along the cut on my arm, now just a tiny scar. I remembered the nettles and thought of Him. My ideas of kindness vanished.

I wanted Him to disappear.

I wanted to be free of His presence forever.

I wanted to walk home from school and not fear the potential of being followed.

I wanted revenge.

I wanted Him dead.

His gang could survive. He was their lifeblood. They would be useless without Him.

But He had to go.

I remembered my instinct when the first nettle stem dragged slowly across the back of my calf, recoiling from its first whipcord snap.

I wanted to kill Him.

I wanted Him to know that I would kill Him.

What would I give for this simple request? Would I give myself wholeheartedly? Would I give the lives of my parents? No, that could not be.

If my desire was to be rid of Him, it made little sense to exchange those I loved.

Would I give something lesser in exchange for His removal, His disappearance? What could I give?

I stared into the stone.

The happiness of home? It was a strange, alien phrase. It certainly wasn't something I'd have thought of myself.

Would I trade the happiness of home to get rid of Him? His actions and violence coloured my days. Home was not a happy place when He existed, as I brought back the sadness He burdened me with. Home was safety but not immunity.

Yes, I would give that. How could an unhappy home be worse than His all-encompassing presence?

Leaves lifted from the ground in swirls, giving shape to the wind, almost like a person. I stood forward from the rock sharply, aware that I had been daydreaming and that autumn darkness was approaching. The leaves dropped suddenly to the ground. I thought little of it afterwards.

Such fantasies were common when I was young.

◎

I hadn't planned to see Dad on my trip. This was merely out of practicality, as he lived reasonably far away with his new partner and was tied down by his job at the hospital laboratory. But he messaged with his usual keenness to meet, one that always filled me with gratitude. I agreed, and on the second day of my stay, I told Mum that he was going to visit. At first, I thought we could use his car to take us far out of the north side of the peninsula. But I thought again of the scrubland behind the motorway and how I wanted to keep photographing it. I still had several shots left in the Polaroid camera

He arrived early and happily stepped through the doorway of the house he had spent most of his life living in. He was a natural fit for the hallway, his body moving around the space with the sort of confident knowledge only gained after spending many years living somewhere. He even put a bag down exactly where he used to.

His movements changed the space, throwing it back into the childhood I quietly longed for before secondary school. It made my eyes dizzy with nostalgia. I choked down the moment with a cough, thankfully put down to smoking, which both my parents knew I had taken to since moving away.

My sadness turned quickly into a spike of directionless rage. The past was brought violently into the present with Mum's partner entering the hallway. I could sense Mum's polite awkwardness. The two men exchanged pleasantries, before we quickly made to leave. It felt like a different world to my childhood.

Dad asked where we were going, and I broke the news that we were walking into the marshland under the motorway. He wasn't happy. It wasn't so much the close proximity – or even the lack of adventure – that curtailed his excitement, but the place's renowned dirtiness, which he hated. Anywhere potentially dirty made him uncharacteristically fusty. It came from working in the sterile laboratory.

I insisted that I was visiting it for work, and that this walk was vital to its completion. He obliged.

We wandered out after he spoke quickly to Mum about how things were, and I fell further into being a child again. Dad wanted to know why I looked so thin, even though I had been thin for years. I could feel his eyes darting around, and before we left the road to walk towards the marsh, he insisted on picking up his pair of binoculars from the car. Being a keen birdwatcher, he wasn't going to miss the opportunity to spy a few warblers in the reeds.

Our conversation flowed easily as we made our way down the adjacent road and towards the start of the curling path alongside the motorway's slip road. He asked me if I was eating enough in London, my slender body suggesting some secretive poverty shrouded from view for the preservation of dignity. His assumption wasn't entirely wrong.

I could see that he missed me a great deal, just in how happy our conversation made him. I missed him too, just as I missed Mum. I hated being away from them, even if their own separation was never something I could accept. I hated how my work forced me away from the area, no matter the positives of London, and I especially loathed the industries for all locating themselves in the capital.

Little could Dad have known that as a child – and, indeed, in some moments of mania as an adult – I believed I had really sacrificed the pleasant home with him and Mum in order to rid myself of a bully.

He stopped to look at some insects on a plant, and I noticed with sadness that I was now taller than him. It was a realisation that he was shrinking into old age and I was still climbing towards mid-life. This difference in size made me want to hug him tightly, partly in the hope that it would somehow shrink me back to a childhood height, when I could hide from the world in his or Mum's arms.

He turned and used his binoculars to scan a patch of gulls feeding on the field. He was sad, as there were no Mediterranean gulls to spot. We carried on, looking towards the school on the other side of the field.

Seeing the school reminded him of a few stories from his time there, which were mostly happier than mine. One story in particular made me laugh. It involved a Geography field trip in which the teacher, having accidentally knocked the bowl of his pipe off while emptying it onto the motorway, had made the bus stop on the hard shoulder while the boys in his class had to get out and search for it on the dangerously busy road. He remembered as well that I had trouble when I first started at the school, though he couldn't recall the details.

He was still unhappy about our current location, wishing we could have gone to Burton further down the coast. As the sky fled behind the motorway his footsteps became edgy, as they were walked in fear of something unpleasant on the tarmac.

The marsh was thick with life and the pylon I had decided to photograph gleamed. The fence, designed to prevent wandering nearer to it, was unlocked, its gate swinging back and forth but blocked by a mound of long grass. Dad cried out as he saw I was straying from the path, telling me to watch where I was walking.

He was looking further into the greenery of the marsh where a number of waterfowl were wading. His need to call out every bird in sight hadn't changed, echoes of his voice travelling from the metallic bridge as I crouched down to take the photo. My camera flashed as bird names floated down to me.

I thought this image of the pylon captured the detailed nature of the area – proof, if needed, that it was not some barren place but a living, breathing ecosystem, growing in between the structures of us all.

I caught up with Dad as we crossed the footbridge. It still possessed the unusual faux-tarmac carpet on its walkways that resembled sandpaper. Graffiti scarred the pale blue metal of the sides, though it was almost all illegible.

I wanted to take the old desire path again through the vegetation under the motorway, but Dad insisted on walking the longer way round on the official path. We spoke for a bit about Mum's move, as well as his new house and partner. I tried hard to conceal my sadness.

We stood in the heart of the motorway's artery and I showed him my Polaroid photo, which had finished developing. He laughed at how absurd his son had turned out, taking Polaroids of pylons, yet clearly also happy about the eccentricity. I think he could see some of his own character in me. I looked at the binoculars hanging around his neck and noted the same eccentricity. We were unmistakably part of the same line.

On the walk, I thought little about my time hiding under the motorway, only really considering it when fully under the concrete flyover. Perhaps part of the gift of memory is not in retaining everything, but letting those unhappier instances decay. Bad memories make excellent compost for nourishing the good ones.

I was glad of our little walk, and knew that, with such close proximity to the house, it would spell only a short time together. But the condensed moment made it more worthwhile. I thought he would drive back to his home in Cheshire with a happy sense of our time having been well spent.

We wandered a little further into the marsh before we accepted it was time to head back. He had to leave anyway, as there were plans set for the afternoon, a meal in Chester at an Italian restaurant that overlooked the River Dee.

Our steps were in rhythm as we made our way back, walking our sadness into the ground and uncertain of anything other than our care for one another. He promised to come down and visit soon, professing his desire to go for another walk around a reserve in Barnes.

He looked at me affectionately as we stood by his car saying our farewells. We were both falling back into our past. I decided to give him the Polaroid of the pylon, on the condition that he would scan it and send it to me so I could use it for my work. It was a token of our walk.

I watched him drive away, stopping by the tree at the top of the road before turning off and beyond. I felt a sting, recognising the goodbye as an echo of an earlier one. I missed him painfully all over again.

I felt older than I ever had before.

◎

The end of my first month in school was in sight. My surprise at having survived was palpable. There had been further incidents of violence involving Him and His gang, though only one was as severe as those first two incidents with the nettles and the craft knife. I kept count all the same.

On the last school day of the first four weeks, the gang became agitated by my refusal to acknowledge them as they rained a flurry of blows upon my pale arms. Their eyes were wild with anger, and yet behind them was a strange emptiness which expressed their own confusion as to why they were attacking me.

Writing had hurt that day, as He had delivered a particularly clumsy blow to my wrist. The pain was bad enough to consider going to a teacher, spinning potential stories in my head of tripping and falling down some stairway. But I let the pain ebb with each copied note and sum.

I was glad the weekend was near. In spite of regularly visiting the motorway and The Breck, I was happy to be away from the collection of rituals I had acquired to stay safe. Few questions or voices had arisen during my time in these places since my first encounter with the stone. It seemed there was nothing else left to say. I sat next to Grannies Rock after school or the motorway at lunch time in a sort of quiet awe.

When under the motorway, or sat on the dark land of The Breck, I was almost forgetting Him. It was as if I knew He was taken care of.

The weekend was a welcome break, especially as the previous one had seemed so empty and had possessed an unusual atmosphere which I could not understand.

I had asked if we could go to Loggerheads again, but Mum and Dad didn't seem to be talking. I woke up on

Saturday morning and soon asked Dad what we were going to do that day, hoping he and Mum were talking again. He professed to have few plans, but did say we – he and I, that is – needed to go for a drive in the morning, which I was pleased about. I enjoyed watching the world from the position of a car window.

Dad looked worried. His face was no longer able to hide his unspecified sadness. As soon as this plan was suggested, there was a sudden urgency, as if this drive meant everything in the world. A rare bird perhaps, I thought, that could fly away at any instant. A small, brown blob sat on a fence far away, crowded by hundreds of other camouflaged men with binoculars and telescopes.

I hurried to get dressed and was quickly ready, wearing my favourite black Adidas three-stripe trackies and a T-shirt with a Tardis emblazoned on it. I asked why Mum wasn't coming, but Dad did not answer. I assumed she was busy, it not being unusual for her to stay in the house and receive phone calls from work even at the weekend, or take Nan to a garden centre.

I sat in the front of Dad's car, which felt unusual. Everything at once seemed strange. The sacrifice for Grannies Rock was soon to be fulfilled.

I always felt smaller in the front seat. It made me feel tiny again, and, with a month now completed in the school, I was clinging to almost any aspect that I felt kept me a child. The drive was not far, just to the coastline of a once-famous seaside resort. It was now a ghost town, dominated chiefly by a supermarket.

I had seen many photographs of the resort in its heyday, especially of its tower and ballroom. Mum often said that Granddad sang in both before they were destroyed by fire and council negligence. Even the great art deco swimming pools that had defined the resort were gone. We had a photograph of one particular swimming pool hanging on a wall at home.

Dad parked next to a grassy husk where one of these pools once was. Uncertainty flooded my thoughts as we stopped – perhaps we had stopped for him to scan the patch of gulls that lingered in the green craters. But he had no binoculars with him, and I felt worried. He had brought me out here, away from Mum, as he needed to talk to me.

Dad said that he and Mum both loved me very much. I became even more guarded, and felt the need to go back home. There was a frost growing over us as he took deep breaths to continue. I imagined myself escaping from this moment, whipped by green stems and lying nettle-struck in total avoidance of everything.

On he continued, with a fragmented story of how he and Mum were separating, each point grammatically marked with a plea to not feel it was my fault. But it *was* my fault. I had exchanged this, casually and naively. I had given something that wasn't mine to give. I had given them to Grannies Rock.

He and Mum had been having difficulties. He was going to move out. I could not imagine Dad living elsewhere. I looked into his face but was met with an equally childish look. It was unnerving. He had turned briefly from a parent into a peer.

I asked him why. He shrugged, saying these things happened all the time and that they would make sure I was alright. I knew this to be true. I see so many images from this moment, and have so many questions still. Only Grannies Rock understands.

I sat still, wishing I had some distraction as my body jittered with worry. He reached out a hand and let it lie on my shoulder. The block of flats and the sandstone rocks of the hill next to the waterfront dissolved. Home was disappearing. All that was left was the motorway and The Breck.

Dad was still talking, but I was no longer listening as guilt consumed me. The car felt like a tomb. There was one final apology and a promise that things would be alright, before he started the engine again and we slowly made our way back to the house.

The beach and its concrete sea defence changed quickly into the mesh fences of a golf course, then a church, some houses and a road which led to the school, before finally the familiar dark stone of The Breck and our road. Mum was waiting for us as we arrived and immediately began crying, hugging me tightly as soon as I was close. She apologised too, but all I could think of was Grannies Rock.

I saw Mum's eyes and Dad's torso as sandstone, even the walls of the house and all our possessions were sandstone. Its orangey dust formed a ghostly mist in the air. It was the sandstone of The Breck, taking everything in its crumbly grasp. I stayed in my room for the rest of the day, barely able to move.

The day turned to night and I knew that dinner would soon be ready. I had avoided lunch, despite both my parents worrying about recent physical changes in me – I'd lost a great deal of weight since starting secondary school – but they had allowed it to pass, considering the circumstances.

We didn't speak as we ate, letting the television fill the void with quiz shows and updates on the latest hunt for the perpetrators of the terrorist attack in America. I moped back upstairs without a word and lay on the bed.

The moon was in the sky early and the streets glistened in its glow. I had torn up my household, torn it up so that I could be rid of Him. I hated Him. I wanted to fill His pathetic body with lichen until His skin turned grey.

I looked towards The Breck from my bedroom window, the rain falling with the night, darkening all. I could only see the old schoolhouse and the trees crowding around it, lit finally by the septic yellow of the street lamps of the road.

For a moment, I could have sworn that The Breck was satisfied.

3

We were called into an unscheduled assembly the following
Monday. Trepidation mixed loudly with curiosity. Time had
frozen over that weekend and suddenly started up again.

It was pouring with rain, and I felt terrified to leave the
house that morning, as if it might not be there when I got
back, washed away on a slurry of rainwater and sandstone.
Dad hugged me with such strength as he left that my arms
ached afterwards. The events of the weekend coloured
everything from then on.

Mum left the house quickly too, after an equally strong
hug, and I sat on the carpeted steps of the hall, tying the
awkward laces of my stocky black shoes. All the while, I
looked at the photograph of the old public swimming pool
on the wall, running over the talk that had unfolded next
to its remains days earlier.

It was only when finally marched into the unusual
assembly and forced to sit on a rigid plastic chair that I

thought more about the other half of this unconscious bargain I had made, the only silver lining. His days were numbered. I had given too much for Him to live.

The headteacher walked in and stood behind a small wooden podium. His presence was foreboding. I hadn't seen him since our first assembly, the day I was stung with nettles. He had vanished from my mind, such was the alarming violence of that day and those that had followed. Now he stood before us like a mythical figure, imposing. He was tall with light grey hair and a face heavy with concern, brows furrowed deeply with worry.

First, he said he was disappointed in our year. He was disappointed with us for two reasons which shocked him. I rolled my eyes in a way I thought was unusually adult. As if the school's rules held stock with anyone. I was battered and bruised every week. His rules meant nothing.

Since the events of last month in America, the headteacher told us, there had been a rise in racist graffiti. He said there was no place for such racism in the school, or such vandalism. If he or any teacher caught a student writing anti-Islamic graffiti, or graffiti of any sort, they would be immediately expelled.

He was talking specifically about the particularly violent graffiti now covering various toilet doors, though he hadn't mentioned it. I thought perhaps He had done it with His stolen craft knife, carving nasty messages while hidden or bunking. It had to be Him.

The other news from the headmaster was more devastating. It had come to the attention of certain teachers that boys were leaving their allotted yard and going out of school boundaries. This was a privilege reserved for older boys, and even then there were still sanctions on entry to certain areas, even in school hours. In particular, he noted that no boys were allowed under the motorway or on the marsh footpaths behind the railway during school hours.

I went numb.

Though I had not been caught, I had clearly been found out. My fifteen-minute doses of violence per day were now extended by another hour. There was no way out any longer. I hoped the voice from the marsh would provide support, but there was nothing. Thoughts dissolved into silence, silence into worry, and worry into a void. There was no home, no escape, no realm left to hide in. I was finished.

The slow tramp of feet filled the air. I found myself wandering in the crowd, but soon quickened my pace so I could pick up my bag from the coat stands and scamper off to my Games lesson.

There was a white screaming inside my head, of such searing volume that it reduced all my thoughts to nothing. I was unconcerned about having my senses knocked around on the field for an hour or two. I simply wasn't there.

Where was I to go now, once the bell rang at lunch? It was early in the week, so the violence quota had been reset by the weekend. I was owed my share. A separate morning break was fast approaching. The discomfort of Games felt minor in comparison to what I imagined was coming my way.

The round teacher had found his favourites and his least favourites, and he couldn't resist his competitive streak, violently tackling some of the boys or tripping them up when, by sheer miracle, they were about to do something with the ball. The teacher had been christened with the nickname 'Bully', though it was apparently a reference to his likeness to a cartoon bull from a TV show as much as him being an out-and-out bully.

He had avoided the lesson as usual, along with two of His mates. He was probably saving His strength.

I could see all kinds of future horror. Violence and humiliation stretched out over such a long period of time that it would totally break me. All was possible. My mind darted from scenario to scenario, my distraction even catching the eye of the teacher who shouted at me for daydreaming in his lesson, resulting in much laughter fluttering behind my tired body. I was forced to do two laps of the boggy field as punishment. My chest burned on the lonely run, squelching through rubbish and shit at a slow jog.

Perhaps I could simply run home, admit defeat, tell all to my parents and beg to be moved to another school, or even to have a home tutor like so many of those children had in the 1950s films I sometimes watched with Nan on Sundays.

I imagined the great mansion house of one film, with a famous little comic actor in a flat cap, the narrative of which concerned a boy's kidnapping by gangsters while sneaking to London to see a magic show. I hated the boy. But the point was that he was rich and was taught at home. He didn't have his legs whipped with nettle stems.

I wanted that same loneliness and a small window cleaner as a clumsy friend.

As I trudged around the field, Bully bawling at us as he kept tripping us up in the mud, I thought of another film I had watched a few weeks before on television. It was a black-and-white Western with Gary Cooper, who I loved. In the film, Gary Cooper was at first weak and cowardly but grew stronger, and I was envious of him being a man. I was not a man. I was a child and could never envisage being a man like Gary Cooper. I believed I was destined forever to be a sort of large child muddling their way through the world.

The Mosslands had disowned me. Its silence was deafening like wind on a mountainside. I thought again of Gary Cooper, standing defiantly in the centre of the screen. He was faced with several options out of his situation, none of which were pleasant. He spoke a line which stayed with me. Even now I look back on it as the moment when I had to stop running and face this dry run of adulthood.

*I have to face the man who hates me*, he said, *or die a coward in my grave.*

Would He really have killed me? I didn't think He had it in Him even then, unless by sheer accident. Perhaps if He knew my rotting desire for His own death, He would have changed His mind. I had given the one thing I loved, or at least felt it had been given, and I wanted this one thing in return. I wanted Him dead.

If I could not run away during that break, I would stay and try my best to fight. He and His followers were all bigger and stronger than I was. But I would fight.

With effort, I managed to dodge any potential trouble in the short fifteen-minute break after Games, though it took my last gasps of energy, drained by a punishing morning. As soon as I was seen, even by someone I liked, I would move on.

The next lessons were Maths with Scratch & Sniff and French, with the usual joke about scones, which meant He would have ample opportunity to follow me into the lunch break. I had managed to avoid this on previous occasions through sheer chance, sneaking out and hiding under a stairwell the first time, or quickly and methodically leaving the building.

Then I remembered the knife. He could stab it through my shirt, slash my eyes. I imagined the pathetic blade snapping off inside me. He could entirely rearrange me. All would finally come out if He killed me, and that seemed the more realistic outcome of the unfolding situation. Like the graffiti He so obviously carved into the walls, I was simply another canvas for His hatred. I hoped at least that the slender design of the blade would render its potential for stabbing relatively low.

Such thoughts dropped away with the sound of the lunchtime bell.

I debated whether hiding was still an option. I could manage fifteen minutes at a time, but an hour seemed impossible. I concluded that if I wasted energy on running or hiding, only for Him to catch up with me, I would be in no fit state to try and defend myself. I could not be Gary Cooper facing down those who hated me if I was tired.

I lingered after French, the other boys noticing the strangeness of my presence as if a ghost had wandered into their midst. My disappearing act under the motorway had been so successful that my presence outside of lessons was now something curious. They could not express this curiosity. It was merely a sense of some change.

I was barely out of the door before I felt my shoulders sag with the weight of a large millstone made of flesh. He had spotted me instantly and threw His welcome around me. His followers soon tagged along from their own lessons, leering and jeering.

My body confused them at first. Its wiry, vaguely effeminate, soft structure was the true reason for their hatred, I felt. I was so weak. Their vision of bodies was an ill fit with my gangly limbs.

I began to perform the manliness I had decided was the best option for self-defence; of the sort seen in films, in the other boys, and even in some of the teachers. At first they didn't know quite how to react as we stood there in the damp yard. I saw our reflection in the long windows of the building, my arms held up in defence. We looked absurd.

In many ways, the composition of this memory is like that of an old Hollywood Western, though my impersonation of Gary Cooper was unconvincing even to me. The confusion in His eyes soon turned to joy, the pleasure of finally evoking a reaction, some resistance which would allow Him to raise His violence to the next level.

Yet within this new fiery confidence there was a glimmer of confusion. His suspicion regarding my resistance soon passed as He pushed my right shoulder, peppered with some insults, including a reminiscence of the nettle incident. I was easy to push.

I jabbed His shoulder back as hard as I could, far harder than He had expected. He lost His balance slightly, daring Him to fall and lose face. It was only the unexpected nature of it that caused the effect, as He was much stronger than I was. His followers used it to goad Him on.

The marshland cried out to stop like an outraged parent at their child being naughty, its breeze blowing unusually strong around us. Perhaps I had underestimated myself, but I was soon brought down to reality by two hard pushes from the other boys. Even they were surprised by my actions, staring fearfully at my resistance. The force pushed me over. They were acting as if they were dealing with an unpredictable creature.

Other boys could see that a fight was breaking out. It happened on a daily basis, and was the most popular pastime in the school.

Dozens of boys soon encircled us. I wished they hadn't, but at the same time, a new plan was forming. When these circles of screaming boys appeared, it meant a teacher would materialise too.

He dived onto me and beat my chest hard until He had me pinned. My bag, crammed with damp Games clothes, cushioned my fall, but my neck and head felt the cold, wet ground. I tried to fight back but I was not Gary Cooper.

My fists could barely find any sort of target. My arms were trapped under His weight.

I aimed bites at His face, and eventually thrust my head forward until one of these blows from my forehead made contact, surprising us both with the force and pain we shared. He was dazed but still blindly pummelling my body, which stung and screamed with the pain. An architecture of leering faces filled the sky. The boys screamed and cheered in small, stinging fragments of abuse, aiding us with occasional jabs of their own, maintaining the momentum of the scuffle for entertainment.

Where would their hatred go if they killed me, if they watched me die? Would it trickle down the grid like the blood from my nose, or find endless new victims? His face receded into the flesh of the others as teachers arrived and they smuggled Him away. I could barely stand as the sky returned.

The boys scattered quickly, some giving swift kicks towards me for their own cathartic release. I tried to stand as the profiles of several teachers broke the horizon like giants. I couldn't get up.

One of His blows had clipped my nose badly, which now ran with warm blood. The stinging felt remarkably like the nettle stems, as if one had been slowly dragged through my nostrils like the ring through a bull's nose. One teacher helped me up while simultaneously screaming threats.

I was unusually happy as I bled everywhere. Even with the severe beating I had taken, He had been hurt too. He was not invincible.

A teacher dragged me through the building with my head held back, my shirt dotted with bright red droplets, limping towards somewhere with first aid equipment. I took pleasure in imagining the boys talking together about my new adulthood. I could not contain myself and cackled viciously.

My body turned to hogweed.

I was the marsh and the stone.

Laughing.

The walls blurred and the teacher faded into ragwort and lichen.

I drifted from the world and fainted in the chair they propped me up in.

I was utterly pathetic.

◎

It was my final day before travelling back to London. My hands were dirty from sorting my dusty childhood possessions into uniform cardboard boxes, ready for Mum's impending move. They would soon find their way to North Wales, though I wasn't precisely sure where. I felt she was moving to get away from bad memories of Wallasey, but there was also a fear buoyed by unusual stories shared on the town's social media page. It painted a vision of an area gradually filled with small-scale atrocities.

The sorting of my childhood felt like a misuse of the little time I had left in the house. To truly capture the happiness of the past, I would have simply sat watching episodes of my science-fiction programme on VHS.

At first, I was reluctant to get rid of anything. Many of the objects had served to create a miniature world away from the reality outside the house. I looked at fantastical little figurines and books, trying to recall their meaning. They were from a bygone age, lighting flickers of compassion when handled.

In reality, I knew why this cull was mandatory. The removal of my childhood was also a removal of the sadness of previous years. It had soured the homely walls and rusted the radiators, once so warm with the pleasant winter smell of that first heat burning the summer-gathered dust.

Sometimes, catching sight of my profile in a certain light took Mum by surprise, as if I was another version of the man she had built her first life with. She fought this feeling gallantly, and overcompensated to subdue it, which warmed me with a deep affection for her.

I thought my method of addressing the past was easier. Perhaps if I had given Ellen's Polaroid camera to Mum, she too could have locked her memories away in photos and been saved the hassle of moving house.

She liked photography a great deal, just like Dad. On one of her visits to London, I had taken her to an exhibition at Somerset House, all about the 'Working-Class North'. She had admittedly been in a bad mood as we walked through the exhibition because the attendant had assumed the concession ticket was for her as a 'senior', rather than for my student discount. *I'm only bloody fifty-three*, she had said as loudly and Scousely as possible, before walking off.

We wandered around the exhibition, enjoying pointing out the places we knew in the images of Wallasey and Liverpool. She saw some friends she once knew in one photo, and told of how she had gone around with Dad and their gang of bikers to the same clubs that featured in a number of the pictures. In another series of photos, she was happy to see exactly where she, along with Dad and Nan, had often taken me crabbing. It was a photo by Martin Parr, with a little information card next to it saying how it represented the deterioration of society.

We found it funny how people were standing back to look at these images with a sense of the exotic, appreciating them with the same chin-stroking attention we later saw applied to the Rembrandts and Van Goghs in the National Gallery. Mum said she could have made a killing by framing all her photos from the days she and Dad went to the Empress, the motorbike club that held rock nights, or their photos of the stock-car racing at the Tower Grounds. She was right.

Finally, we got to an unusual part of the exhibition. For some reason, the curators had made a mock-up of a 'northern bedroom' from the 1990s. It had garish furnishing, framed football photos, a rail of brightly coloured trackies and a sickly neon carpet. Mum looked at it for a minute or two without saying anything, almost embarrassed in fact, and then asked me: *Is this how they think we lived?*

Even in its messy state, my room was nothing like the exhibition's mock-up. The floor in my bedroom was soon cleared of the junk I had unleashed from the cupboard.

The objects suggested a childhood that had simultaneously ended abruptly and, in another sense, not ended at all. My school had made certain of that contradiction.

I packed the neat cardboard boxes back into the wardrobe one by one. This was and always would be the only room I would ever have, the only one that was truly mine. Thanks to my parents, they had given me a place where, for a time, I had known a world without worry. I was filled with gratitude. I could never repay them enough.

The only evidence of my personality left in the room after this intense stint of organising was a few signed pictures on the walls of actors from films I had liked, and several of my Polaroids, which sat neatly on the border above. They were out of place, threatening to drag the room back several decades. I still had two more shots in the cartridge left to fire.

I washed the dirt off my hands in the pristine bathroom sink, rinsing the last vestiges of the past down the plughole. A vortex of greying water whirled for a moment before falling away.

The sun was strong on that late summer day, and the heat had made sorting an incredibly trying task. My T-shirt was damp with sweat. I wanted fresh air, and it felt right to pay one last visit to The Breck and Grannies Rock as a local.

My belongings from London sat in a neat pile on the floor, topped by the camera. I wanted to leave the house quickly, but Mum caught me on the stairs, offering lunch. I declined the offer, feeling absent from the house already. She was dealing with a poltergeist, chaotically visiting the

household. All children visiting their parents when adults
are poltergeists of a sort.

I told her I was going to photograph the stone again.
Surprised, she asked why, having already seen my
first photo of it. I tried to make amends, saying I'd eat
something when I returned. She still worried I wasn't
eating enough, just like Dad.

The street was radiant. Flowers proliferated in a handful
of front gardens, though most in the road had been paved
over to make room to park cars.

As I walked, I questioned the past. I couldn't really
believe that I had killed Him any more, accepting that the
situation at school and at home had forced my imagination
into overdrive. Perhaps the overt feeling that I had killed
Him would subside for good after leaving. Why it lingered
was beyond me.

The blossom floated down from the tree at the top of the
road. I crossed over, taking note again of the blue plaque for
the climber, wondering whether I should take advantage
of the heat and actually climb Grannies Rock. I put such
thoughts to the back of my mind, like the neat boxes filled
with my possessions now packed away in the wardrobe.

The road was extremely busy, cars passing every few
seconds. I decided to walk to where the road was more
spacious, opposite the house where my grandparents
had once lived, and finally managed to cross. I hadn't
considered them much on my visit. Granddad had died
long ago, and Nan had moved further towards the river
since his death. I thought again of Granddad's story of

the Dread Iron, and how tiring the trip had been. I was starting to rust myself.

The trees from The Breck loomed over the back wall of their garden, leaning precariously due to the steep incline of its slope. I recalled the view they had from the window which I spotted from the road below. The whole of the marsh, and even the hill at Bidston with its windmill and observatory, could be seen in one vast sweep. My memories of it are littered with colourful sparks and bangs, fizzes of neon in the air marking the perfect view for Bonfire Night.

I walked back along the road. A little path ran behind all the bungalows that surveyed the road below. It was a dark path, turned to shadow by overgrowing trees. There was a sharp wind which shook the branches. But the main noise once the traffic died down was the sound of the flag for The Breck preservation group rippling dramatically at the top of the pole.

I walked up the steps, those same moss-ridden stones, to the top for the last time. The sky gleamed through the branches. I noticed new metal benches, providing a comfortable way to appreciate the view over the marshland and the plain leading to Wales.

I was distracting myself from awkward questions. I was not a killer, nor was I an accessory – or so I told myself, with the shaky confidence of a guilty person on trial or a naughty schoolboy caught trespassing under a motorway. I had summoned nothing from the ground. Nothing.

Surely my bargain to end His life had been just another fantasy, a horrible coincidence that, while providing relief at the time, had simply putrefied with age?

The yellow of the dead grass crackled under the heat. The rays warmed my skin quickly and uncomfortably. I would soon burn.

My eyes were drawn to the ground. I prepared to say farewell to Grannies Rock. It had remained as silent as the marshland. Simply being there again after months in London was pleasurable.

The marsh's support was quiet. But if I accepted its support, then I would also accept that I had instigated a death.

I remembered the images which filled my mind the day His death was announced. His body had turned a moon-green, so faded in my mind's eye as to seem almost transparent. Lichen scratched through His arteries, its tendrils and slender green fingers running slowly through every soft, organic wall of His body. Capillaries turned to agonising emerald.

These images overtook the reality of His heart attack and His supposed rare heart condition.

I leaned on Grannies Rock, thinking about the people who found Him. They could never unravel the labyrinth of marshland that filled His body, or understand the power that caused His death. Even now, His remains are under the land with its worms, still devouring His last few scraps of soul. I keep falling into these images. I cannot resist the enjoyment they bring. But they carry guilt too.

I turned to my photographic task. My previous photo was taken from the position of the Uncle Stone, the rise opposite Grannies Rock, so this one needed to be closer. I wanted the murmuring trees to be prominent, angled in such a way as to resemble a green wave returning from the swell, about to crash over the rock and flood The Breck with leaves.

There was a stony probability to this photograph. I stood respectfully as I looked through the viewfinder. Ghosts of letters were visible on the stone's face, though only if observed closely. I knew my photograph would not capture such details, but I knew they were there. That was the important thing.

I angled myself low and clawed my way back through muddy guilt, pushing the button on the camera. Its snap of light killed the moment. The camera spat the photograph out, its image rejected as something poisonous like ragwort or hogweed.

The Breck was aging me. I lay before the rock with the photograph developing on my chest, feeling the occasional itch of a curious ant or jumping spider straying over my body. If I stayed there long enough, perhaps the insects would wrap me in their silken affections and drag me to their trees to join the other dead children who haunted the forest.

I liked the photo when it finally developed. Grannies Rock looked like something from a film set. I imagined the stone being used for sacrifices in pulpy horror films, the sort I made my money writing about. It was possible to believe that soon the leaves would come crashing down on the rock. It's why lying there was such a pleasure. I was waiting for the tide to come in.

I brushed off the grass, not wanting to take anything else with me in case it carried the land's spirit. All I wanted was stored in that blurry photograph. I dared the stone to show me its hanging guardian just once before leaving.

Scream if you like, I thought. This rock is mine.

No one came. No one warned me off.

His darkened eyes and bones filled my thoughts, but only for a moment.

With a final look towards The Breck, I was not looking at some past quarry or forest of childhood's rebellion, but at the last echoes of home.

All was white for miles around. The view had been monumental and yet empty, rendered a blank page by the weather. The unforgiving wind, itself suspiciously strategic, had battered the group. It had forced them to turn back, regroup, and try again for the peak of the mountain. They had neglected to obtain the regular permit for this path, desperate to see its heaven-sent view across the roof of the world. But now there was only a frozen void.

The last pair, found afterwards by the Danish, had reached the summit. But they had paid the price, already ordained some years previous, many thousands of miles away. The cold was beyond description, as sharp as the bright crags that surrounded their climb of the Abruzzi Spur.

They had been ambitious, taking the impossible north-west route to the peak. Already it had defended itself, sweeping the climbers' determination away before it returned with the slight warmth of the lower depths.

The leader, impassioned and skilled, was maddened with determination, as if his whole life had been given for this moment. Leading a different group, he went further and further up the various camps of the mountain's dangerous route.

Their eyes felt slashed by the ever-increasing storms, even with visors down. The white was all.

There was only the ascent. Any other direction was impossible to consider. Crevasses and voids into the mountain's heart threatened all around.

A day passed before two tried to make the final venture. Only one made it at first, leaving the other to sleep quietly in the snow. Two more came out of the beyond like ghosts.

The trio soon conquered the rock, even if it had sealed their fate in ice.

In that moment, the climber, faced with a view seen by so few, was not thinking of his position on the mountain. He was thinking of the other rock, the one that had promised him this vision so many years before.

His body, already shrinking with the cold, felt childlike, marked by searing pain that swelled through his limbs with greater and greater current. The lack of oxygen made it seem like a shining dream stretched over all horizons.

He was only a teenager when climbing his first rock; the Grannies Stone, as he had called it. He could not help but feel thankful to it, for fulfilling its end of the bargain. He had finally made it to one of the great pinnacles of existence. Even if not quite the mountain grave that had buried Mallory and Irvine, it was the harder climb, the more deranged structure that seemed to fold its stone back around and continuously remake itself with sheer walls and razor ice.

Now the descent was threatening. The storm pushed with all its strength against the climbers, if not threatening them with a fall, at least seeping into their bones and freezing them.

He thought of the fate of his colleagues, left at various points down the incline. His climbing partner, who had faltered at that last sheer segment, was still asleep in the snow. The body was curled into a half-state between living and dying. The cold threatened to suspend existence but, in exchange, take away its warmth and allow it to continue only as an icy spectre.

As a young man, he had never thought of what would happen after this great victory that was promised to him. It was only the peak that had concerned his youthful mind when he wished hard and the stone of his childhood had answered. He had only asked for a one-way journey, a singular route that, all those years ago, was all that would satiate his need for moving upwards. And now his view was a delirious white.

Others had returned to the last possible encampment. Once assembled there, they knew they would have to wait for the storm to subside. Pain was growing like a fungus within. His blood was turning to ice, pumping out the same lichen and moss that had covered his sandstone childhood. His body staggered to a deathly halt at even the slightest sign of resistance. Joints were immovable mahogany, stuck and threatening to splinter as he was laid down.

The view from the top of the mountain had been like a beautiful Medusa, turning him to stone. Yet the process was not instantaneous. Instead, time was slowed, so that every second felt like a lifetime of torture. Every bodily function was haunted by pain, every process a struggle against the environment.

He heard the mumbling voices of the others rendered with such a low resonance that they may as well have been underwater. They were arguing through their own pain. What were they to do?

Days passed as the opportunity to descend shrank with their hope. The storm lessened but the wind increased, cutting through their tents with the biting resilience of a ravenous creature. He could barely stay conscious, such was the pain. When lost, he was filled with dreams of climbing; of walking along Breck Road, now seen only in a strange vision in black-and-white, as if the cold had drained all colour from his memory.

What had he offered in return for that indescribable view of the world?

He tried to mumble, to ask the question, but the words fell in the shivering air. His lips, charred from the freeze, stung him into silence. The voices also faded. They too were in agony, and burdened with a heavy guilt that even he in his dying state could recognise. Soon he knew that days had passed, realising that his body had barely moved.

He returned to the world once more as he felt a touch on his face from a gloved hand. It felt like he was being caressed through inches of metal, such was his growing distance from life. He barely heard the words spoken to him, nor discerned who had spoken them. Vision was now a thing of the past. They were apologetic words, he felt, but he faded once more and forgot about the drifting goodbye. The other climbers knew their fate if they stayed, knowing their strength could not carry his weight back down the mountainside. One by one, kitted up for a final escape, they left.

He knew he was alone in those flashes of unusual clarity that precede death, but found his mind wandering when breaking through the torment that burdened him. The cold accelerated his thoughts, filled with blurry visions of his past.

He thought of how simple it would be if his mind somehow detached itself from the sickening corpse that trapped him. Opening his eyes stung, so he kept them tightly closed, as if shards of glass cut their sides. Soon he closed them with the express intention of not opening them again.

The cold still cut through, as if fine grains of sand were blasted invisibly through the air, scarring his body with minute abrasions. The agony brought him out of his deathly dreams but reality seemed unrecognisable, the darkness within his eyelids morphing into alien shapes.

All that was left was the cold, yet the thought of the peak kept him alive. Its cost played on his mind, shimmering on the divide between existence and oblivion. The pain was so great that he let out silent gasps, knowing there was nothing else to do; to become one with the place that would preserve him.

This was his exchange, he thought. Nothing was given for free. Such terrain did not know the difference between good and evil; it simply was. Questions of morality were deeply human, but they were not part of the mountain's sensibility.

What strange satisfactions he found in himself when that realisation was finally reached. He knew that his blood was now too heavy to move. Limbs died silently of their own accord, attached to his torso like the dead branches of a tree in need of pruning. He would not see spring again, nor The Breck.

Snow fell on the camp, scattering outside the tent. He wondered if the others had reached safer places, or whether they too had been part of his sacrifice to see the peak. He was unsure whether they had just left or had been gone for days. It bothered him little as the pain overwhelmed his emotions and filled his mind with the final white light that only those who have experienced the truth of the freeze can know.

It occurred to him that the view he saw hid the reality of the world beyond. Maybe this was simply a mountain of the mind. Perhaps behind the white canvas lay not the rocky wilderness of the Karakoram, but the green marshlands of Wallasey and the Viking peninsula where he first climbed.

As death clambered into the tent, the climber thought finally of the stone. He faded into the white, a last ounce of pain bringing him sleep. In that final vision, the stone of his mind's eye seemed taller and more powerful than all of the range around him.

Then the mountain was quiet. No one was left.

◎

My memory distorts what happened after my fight. I was concussed from the fallout and I know that Mum picked me up early from school that day. She was incredibly angry and confused by what had happened. It was the first time anything like that had occurred, and it was out of character.

How could her gentle boy have been in a fight? It was everything she and Dad had worked away from. I could not explain the incident, but I do recall stammering about Grannies Rock, dismissing the stone for not helping and betraying me. She and Dad later put it down to concussion.

After a phone call from the head of the school house, it was declared as simply an effect of an issue at home, exacerbated by anonymous bullying.

His family had been informed too, after someone finally snitched on Him, though it was clear out of the two of us who the culprit really was. I knew it would make little difference. In fact, it was really my worst nightmare. This was exactly the situation that allowed an escalation of such things, especially when the people involved cared little for the school's authority.

A shallow light entered my eyes the following day and my parents agreed to keep me off school for a while. I was so grateful that I couldn't hide my gratitude enough, further raising their suspicion that I was either ill or not telling them the truth. Few words can describe the pleasures of being off on a school day. I daydreamed while sat on the couch, hoping for a film to come on, and watching endless episodes of the old science-fiction show I loved on video.

My mind wandered to the marshlands. Had I put too much trust in the voice and faith in the questions that arose when near the reeds of the Mosslands or the stone of The Breck?

What would happen when I went back to school later that week? I could only envisage it being worse, and that any rebellion against His will would be met with a debt of punishment owed. Perhaps, with the teachers watching more closely, He would perfect a more psychological torment.

I wallowed in those hours, thankful to be alone in the house. The peace was overwhelming, as if I had just been through some drastic medical operation. It was only broken later that evening when it became apparent that Dad was not back at his usual time after work.

I asked Mum about his absence when she returned. She sat on the sofa, watching the news. At first she didn't answer, but then she sighed and replied. She said he was sleeping elsewhere that night and it was probably for the best. All I recall are her eyes and the devastation within them.

Tears threatened behind her glasses. I changed my position on the couch, unsure what to say, and placed my sore head on her lap. She let her hand rest gently on it and all was still. We continued watching the local news, avoiding all else.

A day or two after, I couldn't maintain the need for rest, so I had to return to school. I could barely bring myself to get dressed. My blazer was torn on the shoulder by the scuffle, but I mechanically fell into the daily routine and made ready to leave.

I was worried about other things, not so much the situation with my parents or even what possible danger and humiliation awaited me at school. I thought instead of Grannies Rock and my time under the motorway.

I could not go back there any more, and I felt angry towards it. I was tricked, duped into believing in a better world, and most importantly, had given the only thing I truly had. I wanted to smack the concrete pillars growing out of the marshland.

As I walked up the hill, I watched The Breck's trees sway and was overcome with a burning hatred. I wanted to set fire to it and watch the vegetation crackle under the flames.

As I walked by the playing field, I noticed a strange cordon set up on the grass. Blue-and-white tape marked out a rough square, though no one was nearby except the odd schoolboy looking at the ground within it. The grass around had been heavily disturbed, the mud torn up by many feet and clearly also the wheels of a vehicle or two. It was curious, but I paid it little attention.

The mood was sombre as I entered the gate and milled around groups of acquaintances, huddled in various small packs to fend off the cold as we waited to be allowed into the building.

Boys gave me strange looks. I was jittery still, looking nervously around in case He appeared out of nowhere.

He was never usually there anyway, often defiantly smoking somewhere. But His absence felt different that day, not least as several of His gang were present rather than following Him obediently. The atmosphere was at odds with the usual chattering rebelliousness of the yard. Everyone was on their guard.

The teachers, waiting by the door like statues, wore worried faces as if expecting a riot. The usual strictness of making us line up in classes was for the first time not adhered too. Something was decidedly wrong.

As we walked through the building en masse, it became clear that something was off. Our year was marched straight into the assembly hall rather than our form classrooms for registration. The usual order of things was usurped, and it caused a rustle of whispering which needed regular shouting down by the various accompanying teachers.

We sat down quickly and the headteacher once again walked in to address us. Twice in a week was almost a privilege. His face looked even more concerned than before.

He began quietly, almost unable to talk. He first apologised for being the bearer of bad news. He was sorry to have to tell us that one of the pupils, one of our friends and peers, had sadly passed away. His name passed his lips but I knew already. I knew from the day I first ran to the motorway for shelter, and then to Grannies Rock. I had been wrong to doubt the promises made to me by the voices from the soil.

The headmaster advised us that if we wanted to talk about the tragic loss, of someone whose energetic spirit had touched many of us, then all the teachers would be there to support our needs in mourning and answer any of our questions.

He had died of a heart attack, apparently, but was found on the adjacent field in the early morning a few days ago. In a rather conniving fashion, the headmaster used this as a brief excuse to express the continued need to adhere to the rules about not smoking. Other than that, the death had affected him and the rest of the teachers quite deeply. I was surprised his sadness was so earnest.

The other boys looked mournful too, but I had never felt so alive. Relief flooded my body to such an extent that I began to giggle. All I could think of was how glad I was that this boy had died alone on the field.

As I sat there, memories of a dream from a few nights earlier returned. As the headteacher continued his empty and pointless sermon, visions of the field by the marsh came back to me.

I saw a pair of raging eyes, fulfilling a quiet promise. I heard the voice of the marsh summoning Him late at night. He walked to the field in a half-sleep, where He was met.

I saw a violent death, contrary to the reality of the heart attack.

His body was filled with lichen, bones cracking with the pressure of the living greenery.

His legs were tied with raging nettle stems, their stings numbing His limbs as His pallor greyed with moss pumping roughly through His veins.

His skin turned a translucent yellow from contact with caressing hogweed. His whole body was a torture garden. The marshland rose up within Him painfully, aware all the time that it was I who had unleashed this.

My torture by nettle stem was nothing compared to such revenge. The marshland filled His body with the spirit of the Mosslands, until the pressure finally forced His rotten heart to give out.

I saw it all, until finally the spirit left His body limp and alone on the dark playing field.

I coughed, stifling laughter. The other boys noticed and looked at me with odd, unnerved glances. They knew I had been in a fight with Him on Monday, and it would not be long before they started the rumour that the fight had caused His attack. No one questioned why He was out so late, the reports concentrating on the tragedy of some rare heart disease or malfunction.

Relief filled me like the spirit had filled His body, but instead mine glowed. I imagined His corpse, probably so putrid in the marsh air that it had turned into what looked like piles of summer bin bags, rotting and writhing with living things squirming within.

I kept smiling that day, a grin breaking out from the corners of my mouth. Most of the boys were shocked by His death, which surprised me as He had bullied many others too. Yet I could detect one or two who felt a similar joy that He was gone. Many, no doubt, were scarred by their own encounters with Him, and their mourning passed quickly.

The motorway roared by, seen from the classroom windows, though never quite loud enough to drown out the noise of the teachers and boys. I looked forward to lunchtime, considering sneaking out to see the spot on the field again. But the new freedom of the yard, with its low rumbling of everyday abuse rather than His precise bullying, was too much to savour.

The bell rang, and unlike the dread that had washed over me every day since starting, I was relieved. It was the normal schoolboy relief of being away from a lesson.

The yard looked bigger than usual. Most of the boys were still dazed by the news, some reeling from what was their first experience of death.

Then I wondered: what was His gang up to?

His friends would be like lost children without Him.

I wandered around, passing greetings to several friends, now nervous of me. Rumours about me killing Him were rife.

And then I saw them, huddled and confused. Their hands all thrust deep into their pockets, kicking an empty can around.

I found my legs moving of their own accord towards the downtrodden group, and they instantly spotted me. I stopped abruptly just in front of them. At first, I was unsure what was happening. They were still bigger than I was and could have easily continued the work of their lost leader. But they simply stood there aghast, as if they could see the spirit of the marsh and Grannies Rock rumbling through me as my protector.

My lips gave way to the first itching of a giggle, evolving into a long, malicious grin. It was not mine but the marshland's. I could not stop it shining from my lips.

We stood there for a few moments longer, my smile whipping and tearing at them like nettle stems. My retort was more brutal as there was no evidence of its effects. They could pester teachers with their worries about my actions but there would be nothing to show for it. Their pain was inside, raw, and I was glad.

I drifted on and could feel their stares burning at the back of my neck, like His had done in French and other times when He had hunted me. But the stare was not in intimidation. Instead, it was fearful. They were scared.

The day lingered on after lunch, and I soon thought that school could be just about bearable if I locked myself out

of my own body. I was now more marsh than man. Regret
would not arise for a long while.

My parents separated, eventually. That was when regret
truly set in. I cannot forget the look on Dad's face as he
collected his things. Home life was gone. I missed it dearly,
its loss causing me an unnameable inner pain.

I do not know if I am compensating. I do know that
the pain in both parents' eyes tore at me far more than His
death ever could, the body smeared across the field into
mounds of flesh and sod. It still wasn't enough.

The exchange, however, was complete, and the land
had protected.

This was the last day of note at the school in the
Mosslands.

◎

I woke early that morning, knowing I had a train to catch
back to Euston. The sun rose with me, bringing morning
into the room. I loved the beige hue that light created
when filtered through curtains, a shade that had always
comforted me since childhood. It reminded me of happy
days when illness kept me off school, and I lost myself
in old science-fiction films and television. The taste of a
coming cold was deliriously exciting, as it meant staying
off and drinking endless bottles of Lucozade.

It was my last morning in the house by The Breck,
and I wondered whether I would miss it. My memories
were so fragmented that summarising what it meant to
me was impossible.

My Polaroids stood on the border. The past would soon be locked off, but the lock would not be fixed in its place until I had taken a final photograph. I was always overly serious when enacting my own private rituals.

I had already decided to take another of the marshland under the motorway. No teacher could stop me now. I was an adult.

I had packed the night before in anticipation, craving the struggle of London again. But first I needed to take this photograph.

From my window, I saw boys like I once was, walking along the top of the road. I dressed quickly before debating with my Mum. She insisted on driving me to Liverpool so I could catch my train from Lime Street. Her determination for my comfort had never waned in all the years since I had moved out. I eventually agreed, but insisted on taking a photograph before we left, promising I'd be quick so that it wouldn't delay her drive to work in St Helens.

I soon found myself walking to the motorway. A number of boys were walking in that same old uniform. I walked in the opposite direction, wanting to cut around and down onto the marsh road in the hope of avoiding as many as possible.

I spotted one small boy, weighed down heavily by his bag and the obvious sports gear inside. He looked in danger of falling over backwards. It must have been a day of Games for him. I recognised the fear in his reluctant pace. I knew it well.

On the path to the motorway, a group of boys were smoking by the marshy allotments. For a moment, I was reduced to the scared boy with knife-scratched arms and nettle-stung legs. But the illusion died away as I realised my own adulthood via their looks of surprise and nervousness. Perhaps I looked like a teacher. Who else would be walking that path at this time of day?

The motorway was busy with early morning traffic. People were driving to jobs in Liverpool, just like Mum. I could see groups of boys from afar, all gathered and rustling in the older boys' yard, now bordered by a large metal fence which was only passable by the stubbornly locked gate I used to flee through after Art.

I heard the bell ring and noticed how, in spite of the obvious changes to the school, its droning blare had remained the same. The group of smokers quickly stubbed out their cigarettes, walking off over the grass towards the school.

I walked under the concrete, disappearing once more. I was half expecting the marsh to speak, but nothing came. I felt disembodied and ignored, drifting through the colourful vegetation and graffiti, and along the metal of the bridge with its sandpaper tread.

I wanted to capture a sense of the labyrinth created by the motorway, so I walked quickly along the desire path, damp and shining with dew. It was possible to believe that the road went on forever, boarded always by marsh and mud.

It struck me how strange a place this was for someone so young to find solace. As the morning rush hour continued above, the noise it created rumbled loudly. I could see odd zigzags in the mixture of loose gravel, soil and dead plants, clearly made by a dirt bike being driven in sharp turns. The skeletal remains of the burnt scooter had collapsed, the husk lying on its side like the remains of prey.

I held the camera limply in my hand. I wanted to move but could not shake a feeling of sadness. It started in my stomach like hunger, but soon travelled through my diaphragm, until it reached my eyes and brought forth the beginning of tears.

I didn't want to lose this rough old place. I would take an endless lashing of nettle stems, a whole torture of cuts and slices from knives, if only I could have my home back. I would gladly suffer that and more.

Let Grannies Rock turn my body to muddy pulp.

Let the marshland trap me for centuries below its dark soil. I'd be a willing prisoner on the peninsula.

Let my skin burn and scream from hogweed poison.

Anything would be fine, just to be out of this present day. Let my nostalgia be a rising pain, if only I'm allowed to feel that home life, undisturbed, just once more.

I cried under the motorway. The sobs shook my body. I was a lost child again.

I wiped my tears on the arm of my jumper, leaving a wet patch on its blue material, before crouching down and capturing the motorway one last time. I spied the tiny landscape through the viewfinder, blurred by tears. I turned the flash off so the image would flood with the inescapable darkness that the present always possesses when in close proximity to the past.

With a click, my history was banished. I sat cross-legged again like a schoolboy and waited for it to develop. I watched it carefully as the image became one with my view, the two sharing much but becoming more and more distant from each other.

I had completed my task. The past was now in my hands.

I closed my eyes and breathed deeply. With my exhale, the world returned. I bent the Polaroid in my pocket. The noise of the motorway died down for a moment and a strange, final silence descended, broken only by the rustling reeds. The marsh was exhaling too, ready for the next lonely boy.

I walked back to the house quickly, knowing Mum would be in a rush to beat the traffic entering the tunnel under the river. I found her waiting impatiently in the hall. This would be the last time I saw the house, inside or out. I tried to ignore the feeling that this was in itself a significant moment, making a great effort to fiddle and occupy myself with packing the Polaroid into the small notebook which now housed the other photos.

She hurried me along before the realisation of this being a moment struck her too. Her partner was in bed and we were alone. I could barely bring myself to look at the house as we left, staring straight ahead as I got into the car. She mechanically asked me out of habit where to drop me off, knowing already that it was Lime Street. She sorted her hands-free before the loud ringing of one of her customers filled the car, an angry voice complaining about a building set alight by kids in Croxteth. She looked at me apologetically before quickly concluding the call. She told me to say goodbye to the house and we both gave a theatrical wave.

The car travelled through time as it rode up the hill. The tree that had always been the marker for spring stood defiantly, as if the whole day had frozen in recognition of my leaving. The Breck glared, and I looked one final time

at the steps and the old walls. The trees followed us all the
way to the very end of the long road and then disappeared.

Mum told me of a Norman font in the church by the
traffic lights. I was more interested in the sugarworks and
the old house that sat huddled and bullied within its nest
of metal pipes.

With some loose change chucked into the toll bucket, the
gates of the tunnel lifted and we sped off into its yellowy
darkness. The walls of the tunnel were dirty, and the light
was murky.

She spoke to me about her new house, her hopes and
fears of being away from Wallasey, and in particular how
she worried about being further away from Nan, who still
lived in the town. She told me I should have visited her, and
I agreed, promising to ring her once I was back in London.

Liverpool appeared out of nowhere, at first behind
high grey slabs of concrete, before taller buildings slowly
revealed themselves around the corner. Mum insisted
on going her own way to the station and parking where
the taxis were situated rather than at the official drop-off
point. She knew Liverpool so well, every side street and
backstreet, every road and house. It was because of her
work, but it was also a skill which I don't think she ever
properly acknowledged to herself.

We parked up as an unexpected rain shower arrived.
The car was angled on the hill, looking up towards the
shadow of the theatre where a number of early morning
drinkers stood near the Head of Steam pub. Mum thanked
me for helping with the packing, and said I would need to

sort the same things into a new room in Wales. I agreed and thanked her for allowing me still to have a room.

I hugged her tightly and awkwardly as we were both wearing our seatbelts, noting how easily we still fell into being mother and child. It was the same with Dad. Nothing could break that.

She said she had a little surprise for me, unbuckling her belt and opening the pages of her chaotic, bulging work diary. To my surprise, she pulled out a shiny photograph, one of those glossy 35mm photos that Dad took dozens of every week in years previous and had developed at the chemist in Liscard.

She and Dad had met to sort through the photographs in the house before I arrived, something they still hadn't done despite having split up years previously. She asked me if I remembered this one. It must have been the day before my first day at school. I was stood in the garden, wearing my uniform for the first time, its jacket and trousers amusingly ill-fitting. She commented on how she couldn't believe how tall I was now in comparison. Then she called me her little man and looked at the photo affectionately.

It was more human than the reflection in the visor mirror. My eyes were light and carefree then. I couldn't recognise the boy any more. I would tear the photo in half later, unable to allow it to exist. It made me feel simultaneously alien and homesick.

She handed the photo over and I held it for a moment before dropping it sharply, as if the image stung to the touch. But I picked it up quickly and grasped it firmly, thanking her before putting it in between the pages of my own notebook and saying a final farewell.

I thought for a moment about the stinging sensation. As I stood outside the station in the approaching rain, watching Mum wave tearfully and drive away into the city, the feeling faded just as quickly as it had appeared, as with all things.

'Poets claim that we recapture for a moment the self we once were when we revisit some house or garden in which we lived when young. Such pilgrimages are extremely hazardous and they end as often in disappointment as in success. Those fixed places, which exist along with the changing years, are best discovered in ourselves.'

— Marcel Proust, *The Guermantes Way*

# Acknowledgements

My thanks must firstly go to my parents for their support and permission to play fast and loose with some of the real events and scenarios that inspired this book. I cannot express enough gratitude for their understanding.

I must thank Kit, Sanya and Gary at Influx Press for their continued support. To publish three of my books required a huge leap of faith that no one else in publishing would ever have granted, so thank you.

My thanks again to Gary and to Dan for their useful and precise editing which helped make this book so much stronger.

My thanks to Vince for his excellent design work. Having a trilogy of books with the continuity of quality his work brings is fantastic.

My thanks to Ellen for lending me the Polaroid camera used to take the photos featured throughout and for being a wonderful friend.

Thanks to my Nan for our Monday afternoon calls.

My thanks to Georgina and Oreo the cat for being great flatmates and providing an environment where I could work peacefully.

I would not be able to write my fiction without the income of my non-fiction work. I would like to thank the following for their support that has got me through some difficult and tricky months: Sam at the British Film

Institute, Hugh at BBC Culture, Robyn at BBC Radio 3, Adam at *Little White Lies*, Jeff at Powerhouse Films and Tim at Private Motor Club.

My thanks to the following for their continued support, friendship and generally making the horror of life online more bearable: Andrew Male, Robert Macfarlane, Paul Scraton, Benjamin Myers, David Southwell, Clive Judd, Lauren Elkin, Andy Miller, John Atkinson, Alecia Marshall, Matt Lloyd-Rose and the guys at Folk Horror Revival.

Finally, my thanks to Caroline for her love and support. It may have been support from afar due to Covid but it is appreciated infinitely all the same.

Influx Press is an independent publisher based in London, committed to publishing innovative and challenging literature from across the UK and beyond.

Lifetime supporters: Bob West and Barbara Richards

www.influxpress.com
@Influxpress